Born With The Mark

Mark

Raylin Ramsay

Disclaimer

Any similarities to real places, events, or persons is coincidental or used fictitiously and not to be construed as real.

Dedication

For my Dad

Thank you for being my hero and always being there when I needed you.

For Jason

Thank you for everything.

May you both rest in peace.

Acknowledgment

I would first like to thank God for giving me the ability to do this.

I would like to thank my family and dear friends for their continued support.

I would also like to take this time to send a special thank you to Jason, who encouraged me to get back into writing and pursue my dream. I cannot thank you enough for that. You have inspired me more than you could possibly know.

Thank you to my friend Clinton, who has been there from the very beginning when I came up with the idea for this book.

Lastly, a huge thank you to my best friend Dina for encouraging to keep on this and not give up on my dream.

Contents

Prologue

The queen was seated in the large chair in the living area of her chambers, her long, curly brown hair draping over her shoulders. She wore a long, light blue silk sleeveless dress. She was in discussion with the twin seers Arileen and Asher, who shared the same vision. She was stunned to learn of their revelation.

The servant to the royals had just brought in a red-colored marble pitcher filled with juice and three crystal glasses when the conversation had concluded. A moment of silence followed.

"Milledge, bring Luciana to me. I must speak with her immediately," Helena said.

"Yes, Your Majesty," Milledge replied with a bow and then left to summon Luciana.

"Thank you both for coming to me and bringing this to my attention. You may both leave my chamber; I wish to speak with Luciana alone," Helena said to the two seers.

"You are welcome, Your Majesty," the seers said with a bow and left the room.

Milledge went to find Luciana. He had served the royals since he was a child, but he hated always being told what to do. It ate at him. He felt as though he should be ruling and wanted it all. Milledge was impatiently waiting for the rise of Atlantis. He had befriended Dylian years ago, who is one of the head engineers for gene splicing and had shown Milledge how to splice genes. It was all done in secrecy, as only a few chosen were able to do it.

There were a lot of things that Milledge wanted to do, but now was not the time. He had to play his game right. There was a whole other side to Milledge that only a few knew of—Dylian being one of them. Milledge learned as a child from his father that thousands of years ago, Atlantis purposely went into hiding underwater, surrounded by a plasma dome. Growing up, the truth had never been told to the Atlanteans, but Milledge knew, as the story had always been passed down in his family. No one else would ever speak of it or want to hear of it. He hated knowing the truth.

Milledge proceeded down the marble stairs, went through the second corridor, and turned right. He knocked on the metallic door.

The door opened. "Yes?" Luciana asked.

"Luciana, the High Queen is asking for you," Milledge said.

"Thank you, Milledge. I will be right up," Luciana replied.

Luciana went to meet with the High Queen. As she was preceded up the long marble stairs, she started to have a vision of Milledge talking to someone or something that she could not see in her vision. He seemed very secretive. She said nothing and kept quiet. She had no idea what this meant or why. She also had no idea what he was up to, and she wasn't sure if she wanted to know.

There had been three others like herself, Arileen and Asher, who had visions and also served the royals. They had disappeared over the past fifty years. Some say they went to live among the humans. As for what really happened, no one knew, and neither one of the remaining seers had any visions of them. Now there was only Arileen, Asher, and herself. She wondered if Milledge had anything to do with their disappearances. She didn't like the visions of him being secretive; there was something about him she did not like, but she could not put her finger on it. She had a bad vibe about him but could not and would not show it.

She entered the Queen's chamber.

"Yes, Your Majesty," she said with a bow.

"Luciana, please. We are alone. You know to call me Helena; we have known each other for one hundred and thirty years."

"I am sorry, Helena."

"Do not be sorry. But we do need to have a discussion."

"What is it we need to discuss?"

"I had quite the discussion with Arileen and Asher about a vision that they both have had."

"What was their vision?" Luciana asked.

"As you know, when Atlantis rises, we will help those who have survived the disasters. Interestingly enough, I was informed by Asher and Arileen that two of those survivors are that of your former lover and daughter. Care to explain the secrecy behind this?"

"Helena, when I had been given the opportunity to stay above for two years to study how the humans were developing scientifically, and their different cultures, I had fallen in love. It was love at first sight. Eventually, I did have a child, Jaycenda. I know what I had done was wrong and against the rules. I could not chance not knowing the feeling of love. Jaycenda was born with the 'mark,' Helena. It has been thousands of years since Atlantis had gone under, and anyone that had been born with the mark. With her being half Atlantean, this is extraordinary, as this has never happened. I understand that I had broken the rules and there will be consequences for my actions and for hiding it for so long. I just ask that I at least have the chance to meet my daughter. I have foreseen some of her powers, and they can be dangerous if she does not know how to control them."

Helena thought for a moment.

"She bears the mark?"

"Yes, Helena."

"I will not punish you for this. Jaycenda needs to learn what her powers truly are. Come with me to the labyrinth. We have some research to do."

Helena and Luciana left the royal chamber and proceeded down the hall. To the left, they took the marbled staircase and down to the end of the long hallway until they came to the golden doorway. Etched on the doorway facing was a figure of a Minotaur. Helena opened the door. The silver charm that had an oval-shaped crystal enclosed around pearls that she wore with a silver chain around her neck began to glow bright blue. The labyrinth was one of the few places in Atlantis that did not provide light from the crystals; the only light available was that of the light from the charmed crystal. The light illuminated several feet in front of them.

"As you know, Luciana, only those who are the chosen royals can be down here. Anyone else will be attacked by the Minotaurs. However, you are with me; you will be safe. With this charm, I have control over the Minotaurs. I have not been down here in such a long time. The last time I had been down here I was a child accompanying my father. I hope I can remember the way."

Helena had told Luciana what she had learned about the labyrinth when she was a child before they entered the doorway. She explained to Luciana that the labyrinth had been built under much of the palace, consisting of many dead ends, three levels, and staircases. The Minotaurs were created by the Atlanteans and were placed into the labyrinth to protect the secrets of Atlantis. Originally, there had been five Minotaurs; however, one had been given to the Greeks as a gift to assist them with their secrets. The Greeks had refused to accept the charm that would protect them from the Minotaur in their labyrinth.

When it was learned that humans were being sent in for sacrifice, the Atlanteans were not happy. They had sent Theseus to destroy the Minotaur. When the Minotaur had been destroyed, the Atlanteans made sure there would be no evidence that the Minotaur had ever existed, leaving it as a myth for people to ponder.

They proceeded down the stairwell and down the first hallway. They continued, running into several dead ends. Suddenly, they heard the most disturbing growling noise they had ever heard. It was very loud and close by, and with the little light the charm was providing, they could not see anything. Luciana became frightened and remained still as she felt the hot breath breathing down her neck and heard the ear-piercing, disturbing growl in her ear. Helena quickly turned around as the light shone on the Minotaur.

"She is with me; you are to do no harm to her!" Helena declared.

They heard a small growl as the Minotaur obeyed and stepped away. Luciana, still frightened, looked over towards Helena, breathing heavily.

"We need to go to the crystal; show us the way," Helena demanded to the Minotaur. They eventually came into contact with the other three Minotaurs. On the third level of the labyrinth, after going through many corridors and long stairwells, they reached a very large room. Centered in the middle of the room was a large diamond-shaped crystal stretching from floor to ceiling that cast a yellow glow.

"Place your hand on the crystal," Helena told Luciana. They both placed their hands on the crystal, and suddenly, wind struck them, blowing their hair everywhere as they closed their eyes, gathering the information the crystal would provide them.

Milledge had silently followed them to the labyrinth, hoping to learn whatever it was Helena needed to discuss with Luciana. He was curious about why they had gone down there. He did not dare enter the labyrinth as much as he wanted to; he remembered his father telling him when he was a child that no one other than the chosen royal may enter the labyrinth or, if you were an invited guest accompanying the chosen royal, you would endure a certain death should you enter.

Milledge's father had said that the secrets of Atlantis lay within the labyrinth. He learned of the one who was born with the "mark" of the intertwined half-moons. He had told Milledge of the time when their ancestor Cyrus had once been a royal. Cyrus had become greedy and wanted complete domination; he had discussed taking over all nations with the other royals, and they had agreed, as Atlantis was the most powerful and scientifically developed.

A war had begun, and Cyrus had started to rule the world. However, Arcadian, who had been born with the "mark," had hidden it for so long. With Cyrus' dominating nature, he felt it was time to reveal what he had hidden for so long. Those born with the "mark" are the true heirs to the throne, the High Royal. Arcadian had Cyrus destroyed, and his followers were banished from Atlantis.

Arcadian felt that what needed to be done to undo the damages Cyrus had created was to sink Atlantis to the bottom of the Abyss. When the time came for Atlantis to rise, a new Atlantean born with the "mark" was to rule.

When Atlantis began to sink, the crystal pyramid on top of the palace released a pink, purple, and bluish-colored liquid that went into the sky and surrounded Atlantis in a dome, producing its own sunlight continuously. Besides those who had been banished, some had left before Atlantis had disappeared into the darkness of the Abyss.

Milledge also recalled his father saying some of those who chose to leave Atlantis before it had sunk into the abyss had passed on their knowledge to humans and helped create some of the most mysterious places on Earth. They wanted to leave their mark.

Although not all the Atlanteans knew what Milledge's father had told him, as the past is to be secretive, not knowing the full story behind it. He also did not know the full history of their past. Only what had been told to him from his father. Besides himself, Milledge was sure the only one who knows of the "mark" is Helena, the High Royal. He wants what Cyrus was not able to complete, to rule not only Atlantis but the world. He felt it is his rightful place, after all, he does have royal blood, but ever since Cyrus had been destroyed, his family had since been serving the royals, the descendants of Arcadian.

He had been preparing for this for a long time. He had made sure two of the seers, Baron and Darmel, had been taken care of—they had endured an unexpected death. Enid, however, he had kept around for several years, hoping she would eventually tell him of her visions. But the visions were mostly incomplete, simply glimpses of places and people; however, sometimes she would have an actual full prophecy. He and Enid had once been lovers; she had never expected what he had done.

Chapter 1

It was the perfect summer day. The air was crisp, and the smells of freshly cut grass filled the air. I was getting ready to spend the day with my boyfriend Logan and our friends Nikki and Alex at the lake. I had not mentioned the odd feelings and visions I had been having lately; in fact, I hadn't even shared them with my father. It was something that I had been keeping to myself for the last few weeks.

I had my bag packed for the trip and a picnic basket for our lunch. I ended up making a few sandwiches, added a bag of chips, and snuck some of dad's beer, placing it in the small cooler. I was in the kitchen, adding the sandwiches to the basket and having another vision—a vision of a huge, ancient-looking city, but it ended briefly when the doorbell rang. I snapped back to reality and went to answer the door. It was Logan standing there with his cocky smile and his arm resting against the door frame.

Ah, the great Logan Brooks. He was the high school jock, played all the sports, the one all the girls wanted. He was the most popular guy in school. Why he had chosen to date me was beyond me. We have been together since our junior year and continued to date after graduation. We had both decided to take a break from school for a little while and start college in the upcoming fall.

He had sandy blonde hair with a little bit of wave through it, tall, muscular, brown eyes. Very handsome. As for me, I'm average height, with black hair just below my shoulders that I sometimes like to scrunch to give it a little bit of a curly look. I have a birthmark on my left shoulder that is light blue and looks like two intertwined half-moons that I would simply pass off as a cool tattoo. I have crystal blue eyes, and of course, I always had a problem with guys staring at my fairly large chest.

"Hey there, my sexy goddess!" he said with that cocky smile.

"Um...yeah…goddess…riiight…you know I hate being called that," I said with a scornful look.

"And you think I care if you like being called that or not? You know I will call you whatever I want. You are with me; you are mine."

I rolled my eyes. "Whatever, Logan."

"Don't you ever cop an attitude with me, Jaycenda! You damn well know better than that!"

I kept my mouth shut and grabbed my bag and the basket.

"Logan, will you please get the cooler?"

"Get it yourself! I'll be waiting in the car."

I looked at him in disbelief, but then again, it didn't surprise me that he acted like this; it was the norm for Logan. I walked down behind him to the blue sporty convertible and placed the bag and basket in the backseat. Logan was now sitting in the driver's seat, talking on his cell phone. I went back inside the house and got the cooler.

"Jaycenda, why do you keep letting him treat you like this?" I said to myself. I shook my head and walked out the door, locking it behind me.

"What took you so damn long? You know I hate waiting! You don't ever make me wait! You should know that by now! Don't ever make me wait on anything again! You got that?" He said in anger.

"Yeah, Logan, I got it, sorry," I said in a low voice.

"K, well now off to the lake. Alex and Nikki are already there. We have a thirty-minute drive ahead of us."

The drive to the lake seemed to take forever. There was nothing but silence on the way. I kept thinking to myself, I have been with Logan since I was seventeen; is this how I want to be treated the rest of my life?

Two long years with a stuck-up rich boy who thinks he is all that, and how much I hated being treated the way he treats me. No one really knew; in front of everyone, it was the "perfect" relationship, and I always put on a fake smile when deep down, I was hurting and wanting to break free, but not quite sure how to. I hated the attitude. I hated the verbal and emotional abuse he would give me. Not once would he show some respect for me unless it was in front of our family and friends. I did everything for him and even the things he had asked of me. But for some odd reason, I do love him, if you want to call it love.

He was my first and only boyfriend, and he was the only one I had ever been with. It was Prom night, although I didn't want to; he kept saying things like "Well, you don't really love me if you don't." I should have known better and stuck to my guns, but me being stupid and "in love," I gave in. Yes, I regret it; we were both eighteen when it happened.

We finally arrived at the lake and parked beside Alex's red jeep. We walked down to the beach area. At least this time, Logan was considerate enough to carry the cooler down. But then again, he does put on a show in front of everyone.

"Yo Brooks! What took you so long, man?" Alex asked, running up and high-fiving Logan. Nikki and I smiled at each other.

"Yeah, well, you know, traffic and all," Logan told him.

"Well, 'bout time you showed up. Nikki and I built up a nice lil bonfire, figured we would keep it goin' all day. You knows how we likes to paaarty! Oh, got any foodage? We are on the hungry side."

"Yep, sure do," I said.

We all sat down on the large blanket that was close by the bonfire, continuing conversation and ate lunch.

"Yo, Alex, got the boomage?" Logan asked.

"I has the boomage! Just gotta drive the jeep down here, and we be jammin'!"

Alex was mixed and had an outstanding personality; his skin was mocha, and he had the prettiest green eyes. Not too bad looking. He treated Nikki with the utmost respect, and you could tell by the way they looked at one another that they were truly in love. Nikki was a bleach blonde beauty; she was always nice and, like me, did everything for her man. She had the perfect body; if Logan wanted to call anyone a goddess, it should be her.

I guess you could say I was a little jealous of her. I have seen the way Logan looked at her many times whenever Alex wasn't looking, and honestly, it made me cringe. Nikki had mentioned to me once before how it creeped her out when he gave her those looks. For one, it showed her how he was not only disrespecting me by doing it in front of me, but the fact that Alex was his best friend. And of course, if I were to mention it to Logan…all hell would break loose. Therefore, I never said anything; there have been those times I have learned to keep my mouth shut.

Alex drove the jeep closer to the beach area and started blasting the stereo system. He had a CD mix in and began playing some grunge, rock, and added some pop for Nikki and I.

After a few hours passed, the boys decided to play some football, and I hoped they weren't going to miss, and it flew into the fire we had going. Huh, and whose bright idea was it to have a bonfire in the middle of the day? And on a hot day at that! Nikki and I stripped down to our bikinis and started to catch some rays. I looked over into the fire, and I zoned out; I started seeing buildings crumbling to nothing and water overcoming cities. I was not sure why I was having these; I have been getting them a lot lately.

"Jaycenda! Jaycenda!"

I realized Nikki was shaking me. "Uh, yeah, um what's up?" I asked when I slowly turned my head towards her.

"You tell me. You zoned out and looked petrified, and you are white as a ghost. What's going on, Jay?"

"It's nothing, Nikki. Don't worry about it."

"Bullshit! You can't fool me!"

"Well, the guys are still tossing that damn thing back and forth. How about we go for a swim?" I asked.

"Sounds like a plan!" Nikki said with a smile.

As soon as we entered the water, Logan began to yell.

"Hey Jay! You swim, you ain't goin' home with me! You will not get in my car if you're still all wet and all when we leave here!" Logan yelled. He then came over, waiting for me to come out of the water. When I finally did, he grabbed my arm hard, leaving a red mark, continuing to scream at me for being in the water.

I jerked my arm away from him, turned away, and started walking down the beach opposite of everyone, tears swelling up in my eyes. I was tired of this. Tired of it all. He mumbled something and then yelled for Alex to toss the ball back to him. Nikki came running up to me.

"What the hell was that all about, Jay?" she asked.

I said nothing.

"Jay, I have not seen him act like that towards you before. What is going on?"

"Don't worry about it, Nikki, it's none of your concern."

"Bullshit! You are my best friend! We have known each other since we were like what, three? Don't stand there and tell me it is none of my concern when it damn well is! You are hurting, and I can see it."

I could not hold back anymore; tears were streaming down my face while I told her everything about the relationship with Logan and about the visions I have been having lately.

"Damn girl! Okay, first off, these dream thingies you have been having, um, I dunno, maybe discuss them with your dad or something? That's way outta my hands. As far as Logan goes, he is an ass! You are beautiful and deserve to be treated so much better than what he is treating you! I liked him as a friend since middle school; however, when Alex and I started dating and you two were together, I noticed how he would look at me whenever Alex was not around or paying attention. This I mentioned to you before. It creeped me out, and I thought how disrespectful that was not only to you AND me but his best friend! I didn't like him since. So why are you still with him?"

"Nikki, I didn't know if you would believe me about what things are like when no one is around, and for him to kinda show it today in front of you and Alex makes me feel like now someone would believe me. Oh Nikki, I can't leave him, I do love him, but I get nothing in return."

"Jay, you should have come to me a long time ago about this! And don't stand there and tell me you don't think I wouldn't have believed you. I will always believe whatever you say, even if it is some crazy-ass thing!" she laughed. "And honey, it ain't love, that's for sure!"

"Yes, it is," I said in a low voice, trying to stop crying and sniffling.

"No, it's not. Look, Jay, you are miserable, and he makes you feel that way. Look at what he just did! Whenever you are around your friends and family, you put on that fake smile of yours, which I have noticed, and I must say it has everyone fooled. You must have practiced a good bit."

"I did."

"Well, let me tell you this, when you know, you know, and when you know that's who you want to be with for the rest of your life, no questions asked. Believe me, I know. When I first saw Alex in the 7th grade when he moved here, well, I knew, don't ask me how, I just knew. I felt an instant connection with him before we had even met. I truly and honestly cannot describe the feeling. Every time you look at them, think about them, they bring a smile to your face, and don't forget the butterflies in the stomach! It's a feeling like no other; it's really something, though. It's almost like electricity running through your body every time, but again, you cannot really describe it. That is love, not what you are going through. So, with that being said, can you honestly tell me you had anything like that with Logan?"

"No."

"Then I think it is time you two had a lil talk, and I think you know what you need to do," she said.

Alex came running up to us and wrapped his arms around

Nikki. "Hey sweetness, we are about ready to go; it's been a long day already, and the sun is about to set soon. I am sooo sorry for not paying a whole lot of attention to you today. Logan had to play some ball and needed to talk about something."

"That's okay, babe, it gave Jay and me a chance to catch up on some much-needed chit-chat," she said.

"Um, Jay, you okay?" he asked.

I must have looked like a complete mess. "Uh yeah, I'm okay, thanks."

"You know I am here for you too, Jay, not just Nikki."

"I know, and thank you," I said with a half-smile.

"I must say you have a big surprise in store for you later; maybe whatever is going on will make up for what is happening," he said with a big smile.

I looked back towards the camp area we had temporarily set up earlier that day. Logan was busy putting out the fire and drinking some beer.

"Yo Brooks, you ready to roll?" he yelled at Logan.

Logan yelled back, "Yep, let's roll."

We loaded up the car, and I got my shorts and tee-shirt back on over top of the bikini. The air had a chill in it, so Logan put the top on the convertible.

On the way home, we had silence again. I shut my eyes, thinking of what I wanted to say and what I wanted to do about the relationship. It occurred to me that, to be somewhat happy, I needed to leave Logan. As much as I love him, I needed to do what was best for me. I need to allow myself to be happy again.

Happiness is something I had not had in a very long time, and realizing this now, yes, I needed to break up with him.

I opened my eyes when I felt the car swerve back and forth, hearing Logan laugh as though it was funny to scare the crap out of me, and it made me uneasy.

"Well, well, it's about time you woke up. Almost back to your place."

I said nothing. I wanted nothing more than to get home and take a nice long bath and go to bed. Five minutes later, we pulled into the drive. Dad had the porch light on. I hurried out of the car and grabbed my stuff.

"Whoa there, why are you in such a rush?"

"I'm tired, I want to take a bath and go to bed; it's been a long day," I said as I continued to walk up to the porch with my bag over my shoulder, cooler in one hand, and the basket in the other.

Logan followed me up to the porch. I set the cooler and

basket down, fumbling through my bag to get my keys. He grabbed my hand and pulled me over to the porch swing. We both sat down, I started to rock the swing.

"Marry me, Jaycenda Spencer."

I had no idea what to say, as I was planning on leaving him; maybe now is the time to tell him goodbye. I was getting ready to tell him how I was feeling and how much he had hurt me when he grabbed me like he did. The next thing I know, he was pulling out a small box out of his pocket and opened it. Inside was the most beautiful ring I have ever seen with a huge diamond. I looked at it stunned; he had never gotten anything for me so beautiful, I was speechless.

"Well, are you gonna answer or not?" he asked.

"Logan, we need to talk."

"There is nothing to talk about. You will marry me, and that is final! You are my goddess."

Okay, so at this point, the whole goddess thing again; I wanted to puke. He knows how much I hated being called that, yet he continues.

"I, uh, I'm tired…" He put his finger to my mouth before I could finish.

"Shhh. Say nothing more." He removed his finger, took the

ring, and placed it on my finger.

"Going out of town with my folks tomorrow. I'll be back in about two weeks. As soon as I get back, we will start making plans for the wedding," he said as he got up and practically ran to the car, got in, and drove away.

I just sat there speechless. Everything I wanted to say to him I couldn't, and because I was too nervous to stop him and say anything, I was now engaged. Maybe this was my destiny. Get married and have a family with him. Who knows what is in store for me. It's part of the big mystery of life.

Chapter 2

I finally got up from the swing, finding it hard to believe that just happened. As I walked into the house, to my surprise, there were boxes everywhere in the living room, some stacked on top of one another.

I looked around and noticed some things were no longer in sight, such as the only picture of Mom and Dad; you could tell they were in love. In the picture, Dad and my mother were looking at one another with huge smiles on their faces. She had long curly red hair, the same color eyes as me. Dad was taller than her, his hair pitch black (now salt and pepper color) and looking down at her with the biggest smile I have ever seen him have, other than my graduation.

I looked down at a small box, and there was the picture in the beautifully carved wooden frame. I pulled it out to look at it. I wish I had the chance to know my mother. Dad would never go into detail about whatever happened to her, only that she loved me very much. I was only a few weeks old when she had left. I often wondered what happened. Did something happen to her, or had she just decided to up and leave everything behind? I asked Dad about it, but he still would not say, only to say she loved me very much and one day I will know what happened, now was not the time. It was always the same thing.

"Dad?" I called out.

"Hi, sweetie! How was the trip to the lake?" He asked from the kitchen. It smelled like he was starting to burn dinner again.

"It was fine... Um, what are all these boxes for?"

"We are moving in a few days."

"What? Why? I can't! Where are you moving us to? I mean, why and where are you moving? I'm starting college in the fall...."

Dad looked at me with his big brown eyes and ran his hand through his salt and pepper hair.

"Honey, we are moving to Burnsville, North Carolina."

"Dad, I am not leaving Michigan to go there! What about my friends and Logan? I can't up and leave them! Logan and I just got engaged!"

"You are what???"

"Engaged," I said as I held out my hand to show him my ring.

Dad pulled out the pizza from the oven. He looked like he wanted to cry yet was angry at the same time.

"Sweetie, we are overdue for a much-needed talk, and you are moving with me to Burnsville whether you like it or not. I am still your father; I pay the bills around here. I never cared much for Logan; I think he puts on a front half the time, and my daughter is not going to marry some stuck-up rich kid who thinks he knows it all. However, your friends, and as much as I hate to say him as well, can come and visit whenever they like. Especially the week of December 10th this year; it is, after all, 2025. Big things are going to happen."

"Huh?"

"We will talk after dinner, Jay."

Dad sliced the pizza and put two slices on a plate for me and two for him. We sat down at the table to eat. As I was stuffing my face with the pizza, I was giving him a strange look, not knowing what to expect. But I was also thinking that maybe a move would not be such a bad idea, considering I was wanting out of the relationship with Logan, yet I didn't, not since he proposed and basically stuck the ring on my finger before I could answer. Maybe that was my destiny. But thinking about it more and more, I am fed up and want to start something new. But I will see what all Dad has to say.

After dinner, Dad and I walked into the living room and found our way to the sofa among the maze of boxes.

"So, Dad, what is this long overdue talk all about? Before you begin, there is something I need to tell you; it's rather important."

"Please do not tell me you are pregnant!"

"No, no!"

"Thank God!"

"Dad, I have been having these weird feelings lately that I truly cannot describe, and I have been having these visions/nightmares, whatever you want to call them. They have been dealing with brief images of a city that's more like a glimpse and like no other city I have ever seen. Also, these nightmares that, well, sometimes happen even when I am awake. Seeing buildings fall to nothing, fires everywhere, cities being flooded, and so much more. I do not understand any of this. It's like I am going crazy."

"Jaycenda, this overdue talk... it has to do with your mother and why we are moving."

"My mother? But you would never discuss her before, as many times as I have asked you, why now?"

"It was never really simple to try to have explained it; you would have found it hard to believe."

"Try me."

"This isn't exactly easy for me, you know."

"I know Dad, just spit it out already."

"Look, you are going to think this is all crazy, and it sounds crazy, but it is the truth. The visions you are having, well, your mother said you would be getting them. Your mother left because she had to go back to her home. She told me where the best place to be when everything happens, and that is why we are moving to Burnsville. When we met, your mother, Luciana, took my breath away. It was love at first sight for both of us. However, her time was to be short, not long term. She is from Atlantis. Yes, the city does exist. I didn't believe her at first, but then looking into her eyes, I knew she was telling the truth and what she had given me to pass onto you when the timing was right."

"Yeah, right... and I am a real-life princess. Come on, that is craziness!"

"Before I finish, follow me to the basement. I will show you what I have been saving. Maybe this will prove to you what I am telling you and what I am about to tell you."

I followed Dad to the basement. I hated this basement. It was one of those dense, creepy basements where you always felt like you were being watched. Dad went towards the back of the basement behind the stairs. There was another room down there, however, Dad had always kept it locked, and I was never allowed in there. Dad unlocked the door and switched on the light. Looking around, there was a desk and a chair, nothing else, odd I thought. What was so special about this room was beyond me.

Dad opened the bottom drawer and pulled out a fireproof

safe. Dad opened it up. Inside was this octagon-shaped metal box that could fit in the palm of your hand, a semi-large crystal that looked as though it fit perfectly in the metal box, and a silver metal headband with a teardrop crystal on it. Both the box and headband had the same unusual etchings. Dad looked at me like he was about to cry.

"I have never stopped loving your mother. There have been many times I have opened this over and over again and thought about her. I couldn't show this to you yet because the timing was never right. Now is the time. Are you ready?"

"Yes…"

I sat down in the chair not knowing what to expect. Dad placed the metal box on the table in front of me and put the crystal in the box, as I thought, a perfect fit. Dad then placed the headband on me. He told me to close my eyes and concentrate. I closed my eyes. All I saw was blackness, and then I saw a figure form in front of me. It was my mother; she looked so beautiful, her long flowing curly red hair, and she was wearing a headband like the one I was wearing. She was dressed in a white dress, something you would see in ancient Greek days, with a silky blue shawl draped over her shoulders. She had the most beautiful smile, the same eyes as me. She truly looked like she should be on the cover of a magazine. I went to hug her, but my arms went completely through her. I backed away and just looked at her in astonishment.

"My dearest Jaycenda, I want you to know how much I love you and your father very much. Please don't think that I had abandoned you. I had to leave as part of my duty to the royals. I am looking forward to the day we will be reunited again. Unfortunately, this will not occur until 2025 after Atlantis has risen. Do not fight your father on the move to Burnsville; I had foreseen you somewhat arguing with him over it. This is very important. It is one of the safest places for survival of what is to come. As you are being here receiving this message, then your father is aware of the visions you would have started having. It is part of your bloodline from me to see things or glimpses of things before they happen. Sometimes you may receive a full prophecy. Only a few of us have this power, and we serve the royals. That power is passed on to our children. It is one of the greatest duties that one can have. As of right now, I am only one of the few seers left. I have foreseen you having other gifted powers as well, which for a seer does not have. I have foreseen you tapping into them before we meet again; you must try to control them. It has been thousands and thousands of years since one has been blessed with the mark of the intertwined half-moons. And for you being half Atlantean born with the mark is extraordinary. I will see you soon; I love you and Sam very much, please pass my love onto him." She faded away.

I opened my eyes, and tears started welling up, flowing down my face. Dad removed the headband and placed it back into the safe along with the crystal and the metal box. I, however, could not say anything. We went back upstairs; Dad took the safe up with us. He said there was no reason to keep it locked up anymore.

We sat back down on the couch.

"Now do you believe me?" He asked.

My nose was sniffling, and tears were still streaming down my face. I shook my head yes as Dad handed a tissue to me. I explained to him everything that Mom had told me and that she sends her love. My birthmark on my left shoulder I never thought it was anything special. Until she had stated so.

"I wish I was able to have seen that. Only you can, as being part half Atlantean. I could not see anything. I have tried once but it gave me nothing but a severe headache and heard a screeching noise that hurt my ears. Therefore, I have never tried again.

"Uh, um, so, yeah, well where is Atlantis then? And how come nobody has found it yet if it still exists?" I asked.

"Well, Jay, it is not meant to be found. Only I know where it is, and I will tell you, however, you cannot share any of this information with anyone. You are half Atlantean, and the glimpse of the city you have been seeing, well, I believe that you were seeing Atlantis. Anyway, your mother had trusted me enough not to tell anyone, and I, in turn, trust you. If anything is said, of course, people will start thinking we are crazy. As you know, the Mariana Trench is also known as the Abyss. No one truly knows its depth, and that is where Atlantis lies. Your mother had described to me how it is enclosed in a plasma dome, and a majority of the "UFOs" are actually the Atlanteans watching us. Those Atlanteans are called the watchers. They have been watching us for a very long time, and some, like your mother once had, are here living among us, and no one even knows it. They are far more advanced than we are. I don't know all of the secrets; your mother refused to say, as she was already breaking the rules about a lot of things, telling me about Atlantis, falling in love, and having a child with a human. She mentioned that on December 12th of this year, there will be a lot of destruction."

"Remember in school when you were learning about the Spanish Conquistadors?"

"Vaguely. But yes."

"According to your mother, the Mayan codices contained the actual date. December 12, 2025. The Mayan calendar that many believed was for December 21, 2012. That calendar was to push people to prepare for what was actually to come, whether they chose to or not. It was not meant to be believed as the end of the world. It is to come 13 years after the false prophecy many had believed. The number 13 represents in the Mayans where sacred lords ruled the Earth. Hence the rising of Atlantis."

"Uh, okay. But wouldn't there be some record of it?"

"No, Jay. Your Mother stated the codices that contained the actual date of events were destroyed with many other important documents recorded on the codices by Bishop Diego De Lana, who believed the codices were nothing but superstition and lies of the devil. He ordered all of them to be burned. Therefore, no one would know of the date. The prophecy was passed on to the Mayans from an Atlantean seer. There will be massive destruction all over the world, flooding, volcanic eruptions, weather-changing patterns in which we have been having those, but more so lately, only because of the fact the planets are starting to realign with the sun. When they form the full alignment, it will be much worse, and when the poles shift, Atlantis will rise."

I just sat there; I could not comprehend everything at once. This had been a blow to me. I needed to call Nikki just to talk and get my mind off things. I vowed to Dad I would not mention any of this to anyone. I also decided that I do need this move, and I needed to let Nikki know.

Ring, ring, ring… "Hello?"

"Nikki…I need to talk to you. Can you come over?"

"Sure…did you break up with Logan?"

"I'll explain when you get here."

"Okay. See you soon."

I knew Nikki would be a while before she comes over. Right now, I needed to play some music. I went through my assortment of CDs and found it. Perfect! One of my favorite rock bands. I put it in the stereo and hit play. I started to sing to the lyrics.

After playing my song, I went downstairs and waited in the living room. Ten minutes later, there was a knock on the door, and I got up to answer it.

"Hi Nikki," I said.

"Hon, what's wrong? You sounded terrible on the phone."

"Let's go sit down so we can talk."

"Jay…. what are all these boxes for?"

"That's what I need to talk to you about."

I went on to tell her about what Logan had done and how I did not have a chance to tell him it was over and how dad had a surprise move in store for us.

Nikki was in disbelief. Her eyes started to well up, and she started to cry.

"I can't believe you are moving, Jay! As much as I don't

want to see you move so far away, maybe it is the best thing for you. This is probably in the best with the situation with Logan. Although when we come to visit, you know we will have to bring Logan with us as he would have the money to go down there."

"I know, and maybe it is for the best. I didn't want to go at first, but then I think I need this more than anything. I will call him when we are moved. I don't want him to know about this; he is leaving tomorrow to go on a trip with his parents, and I don't want him not going and trying to stop me."

"I can understand that. You have had a long day; you need to get some rest and start packing. Alex and I will come over tomorrow to help out and spend that last little bit of time we have left with you before the big move. We love ya, and we will miss you. I will fill Alex in on everything tonight. I know you have been through a lot and don't want to talk about this again."

"Thank you! You are the bestest friend anyone could have asked for! I love ya too!" I gave Nikki a hug.

"See you tomorrow, girl! Hang in there!" Nikki said as she left.

I took some boxes up to my room. I started to pack a few things away, but I was already so exhausted from the day I decided to change and go to bed. That night I started to have this dream, although I wasn't sure if it was a dream or if I was actually having a vision. I dreamt I was under water, blackness all around, going deeper, and deeper into the depths of nothingness. I then saw this bubble-looking thing that was enclosed in a pinkish, purplish, bluish liquid that was glowing. I could not see past it; I could not see into it. I then saw a few ships shoot out of it like a bullet. They were so quick I really could not describe them. I wasn't exactly sure where they were going; there was just so much darkness except for the bubble that was before me. Then the dream changed, and I dreamt that I had called Logan and told him about the move and how furious he was with me and that everything was my fault and how dare I accept his ring when I up and moved away. It was not a pleasant conversation. I then saw the most spectacular view of mountains at sunset, and this had made me feel such comfort that I had not had in years, it was very peaceful.

Beep, beep, beep… My stupid alarm was going off. I didn't realize I had the alarm set for 7:00 am. Well up now. I might as well get ready and start packing. I went downstairs to fix breakfast, which, to my surprise, Dad was already starting to make.

"Dad, no offense, but please let me cook; you tend to nearly burn everything, including toast," I said.

Dad laughed, "Well, if you really want to… be my guest; you are a better cook than me anyway."

After breakfast, I got ready, went back downstairs, and we

started packing up the rest of the living room. Dad told me he hired a moving company to take care of everything; they would be here by tomorrow morning, and he and I would be on the road the following day.

It was about 10:00 am when Nikki and Alex had arrived. We took some more boxes up to my room and started packing everything. I pulled out my two large suitcases and packed them up. I was excited about the move yet saddened.

"Jay, Nikki had filled me in on everything. I am so sorry; I had no idea, well none of us did really, had I known, he and I would have gone to blows," Alex said.

"I was too afraid to say anything, Alex."

"Girl, we got your back!" He said.

"Hey, you know how about when we get done here, we go to Chatterbox," Nikki suggested.

"That sounds great! I would love to have one last night out with you both!" I said.

We finished up; everything in the house was packed and ready to go. We headed out to dinner and reminisced over the past few years.

Chapter 3

It was moving day. I had to say one more last goodbye to Nikki and Alex; I will miss them dearly. They are my best friends, and I hope they do have the chance to come and visit. I continued to wear the ring Logan gave me. I had yet to call him. Dad placed the house up for sale and had the SUV loaded with luggage and some boxes we decided to take with us rather than have the moving company take them. We left early morning before sunrise. It was going to be about a twelve-hour drive for us, and Dad wanted to drive straight through with a few stops here and there to stretch our legs.

A few hours later, we stopped off in Ohio to grab some food and gas. Dad had heard about this place called the Serpent Mound that he thought would be interesting to check out on the way. After some long back roads, passing cornfields here and there, we made it, thanks to the GPS guiding the way. We drove up a small curvy hill. We went into the small gift shop first. There had been some interesting gems and such; we got our map and continued over to the mound. I felt this rush of energy I have never felt before, the closer we got the more intense it got. We had climbed up to the top of the tower to get the whole view of the Serpent Mound. It was perfectly made, with seven winding coils. The head of the serpent shape looked as though it is about to swallow an egg. It was interesting. When we got down from the tower, I had this urge to go to the very end of the mound. The tail end was more circular, and I felt the need to stand in the middle of it. The energy was very strong throughout my whole body and then it stopped. I had to catch my breath; it was so strong. I wasn't feeling right and told dad we needed to go. We immediately left and got back on the road.

I was having another vision, more destruction; I wish I wasn't seeing this again; it is almost like torture to see this being played in my head over and over again. I am not sure how much of this I can take. This time I was seeing several volcanoes erupting all at once, black heavy ash covering the sky, lava flowing destroying towns. I woke up feeling like I was on fire and gasping for air. Dad pulled over.

"Jay, Sweetie! Are you alright?" Dad asked.

I finally caught my breath. "Yeah Dad, I just had another vision and this time I felt like I was on fire. But I'm ok. Don't worry about me; I am fine."

"Okay, hon. We have a lot more road to cover; I would let you drive, but I would be afraid to let you if you have another vision again."

"It's alright Dad, I will do a majority of the unpacking, it's only fair, you are doing all the driving."

"Sounds like a deal. I have a surprise for you when we get

there, but don't ask because I will not tell you; you will find out."

"Alrighty then. So where exactly is Burnsville at in North Carolina?" I asked.

"Burnsville is in the mountains; it is near Mt. Mitchell, which so happens to be the highest elevated feet this side of the Mississippi. Remember when I had taken a two-week getaway last summer? Well, I went there to check everything out and to look at some property there. I bought a nice piece of land and had a cabin custom built; I think you will like it. I stayed at a bed and breakfast while I was there. I'll have to take you to this lil diner. The front of the diner during the summer is done up like a garden; there is a covered porch with a willow tree in the middle of the porch, at night it's all lit up around the porch, it's very nice and the food is wonderful. On the inside, it is small but quaint. The whole town is a quaint setting; there are festivals in the town square where the bed and breakfast and the diner are located. I think you will like it. We will be about twenty minutes from town and about fifteen minutes from Mt. Mitchell. We will be in the mountains, and the winters can be very hazardous from my understanding. Now the roads are very winding and curvy. Until you get used to them, you will get a little car sick; I sure did. You may laugh at this Jay, but the cabin I had built, I had a few rooms in the basement built into the mountain; you must go down a long hallway to get there, but it's basically a bomb shelter so to speak."

"Hmmm, okay, so is there anything to do in this town?"

"It is beautiful, but not much really to do. There is no Chatterbox, there is no mall. The folks there are extremely friendly. I think you will be surprised and actually like it there. I know Nikki and Alex won't be there, but you know they can visit anytime they want. If they have problems trying to get down here, you know I will assist them. I know you miss them already, but make sure they are here by December 10th. Okay?"

"Okay Dad. Thank you; I do want to see them soon." I said, hoping he would take the hint that soon would be next week.

"Anytime hon."

It was a few more hours before we arrived. I don't know how much longer I could take singing "99 Bottles of Beer on the Wall" and playing the "I Spy" game. It was fun for a while, but it got old. It did, though, make the rest of the trip seem to go more quickly. Dad was right; the roads were so windy, and I was getting a little sick. Who would have thought roads would have so many twists and turns? I'm not sure if I can get used to it or not. Dad drove straight through town; about twenty minutes later, he turned up this long, windy gravel road and drove all the way up to the cabin. It was beautiful, and there had been a new shiny black truck sitting right beside it.

"Well Sweetie, there she is, your surprise! Go on, check her out, here are the keys."

"Really? Dad! That's awesome! I love it! I love you Dad! Thank you so much! Thank you! Thank you! Thank you!" I said as I hurried out of the SUV and running over to it. As soon as I got to the truck, I was jumping up and down for joy. I unlocked it and got in it to check it out. It had a GPS installed, USB player; it had the works and yes, even chrome wheels, how sweet is that! I played around with it until Dad made his way over.

"So?" Dad asked.

"Dad, I was not expecting this! Wow! How can I ever repay you?" I got out of the truck and gave him the biggest hug I had ever given him.

"Sweetie, there is no need to repay me. I am your father; I love you, and you are not going to pay me back. This is your gift. You need something to drive around in here in the mountains; however, the GPS does not always work in these parts of the mountains. And also, with these visions going on lately, I do not think it is a good idea if you drive alone; I don't feel comfortable with that at all."

"You got it. I promise I won't drive unless you are with me or if Nikki and Alex come down."

"Oh good, you didn't mention what's his name." Dad and I

chuckled at that.

The cabin was beautiful. It sat close to the edge of the mountain but not too close. The foundation was stone, and it had a huge covered porch on it. It had the most spectacular view of the mountain ranges and the valley below; it was the same view that I had in my dream. It was very peaceful. We walked inside; off to the right was the staircase. The living room and kitchen were an open floor plan with the laundry room off from the kitchen. It had stainless steel appliances which I absolutely love and cannot wait to make some awesome meals in that kitchen. There was a huge bay window that looked out onto the porch and the view. The fireplace in the living room was made of river stone. Dad showed me the upstairs; my room was the first on the left; it was huge with its own bathroom.

I am loving this place even more. Dad's room was towards the end of the hall; there was a third bedroom and another bathroom between our bedrooms. We went back downstairs, off from the laundry room was a door, and we proceeded down the stairs and walked down the long hallway. There was a heavy steel door. Inside consisted of four rooms, including a bathroom. Dad explained the reasoning behind it, and that when December 12th, 2025 occurs, we were going to be in here. He made it pretty much an underground shelter that looked more like a small apartment. We headed back upstairs and started to unload the SUV. We were told the movers were not going to be here until the next day, so we had the privilege to camp out on the floor.

After unloading several boxes, I went up to my room. I got the cell out of my purse. I was shaking. I needed to call Logan and tell him we had moved. I know this was going to ruin his vacation with his parents, but I didn't want it to be a big surprise to him when he came back.

Ring, ring, ring…

"Hello?"

"Logan, it's me."

"Oh, hey babe, why you gonna call me while I am on vacation with my parents? If I wanted to talk to you, I would have called you!"

This, of course, made me furious. Like, okay, is he really vacationing with his parents or is he with someone else? Either way, if he loved me, he would not talk to me like this.

"Yeah, well, whatever. I am tired of you being like this, and it's about time I said something about it, and oh yeah, dad and I moved to North Carolina. I am tired of your ignorance, the wedding is off, we are done!" I yelled and hung up the phone.

The phone rang. Caller ID showed it was Logan. I went ahead and picked it up.

"What do you want?" I demanded.

"How the hell do you just up and move without telling me? We are engaged, and you're going to pull this shit with me? How dare you! And how dare you cop an attitude with me and hang up on me! I have every right to talk to you however I want, you deserve it half the time! Thanks for ruining my vacation!" He started to proceed, and for once I cut him off.

"How dare I? No, Logan! How dare you! Listen to yourself, Logan! That is exactly what I am talking about! And why I had hung up on you! You never give me the chance to explain anything. I didn't know about the move until the night I came home from the lake! I couldn't have any other friends other than Nikki and Alex; I was never allowed to do this or that, anything I ever wanted to do I wasn't allowed. You are completely against everything unless it is something you want to do."

"You are too damn controlling, and you always have an attitude! The only time you do not have an attitude with me is in front of our family and friends. I deserve better than that! I will no longer be miserable! I'll send the ring in the mail!"

"You are going to move back, and we are going to have a long damn talk Jaycenda! You are NOT going to leave me, I love you and you love me, and we will work this out! I will see you in a few days. I'm cutting my vacation with the folks short."

"Logan, you are in denial, and I have had it. You did not listen to one word I had said. I love you, but I can only take so much. You and I, we are over. Goodbye Logan." I hung up the phone. I have never felt such relief.

He tried calling back several times. I never picked up. I eventually had to turn the phone off. I felt like a huge weight had been lifted off my shoulders. I had felt a little sad about it, but at the same time I was proud of myself. I had never stood up for myself before, and it felt good.

That night I had been tossing and turning. I have been having the weird feelings again. It was like a tingling feeling all over and then I felt like my body was on fire all over and then cooled like I was in a freezer. I sure as hell did not understand any of this. The next thing I know I am looking around, I was no longer in my bedroom, I was somehow or another in the kitchen. Had I been sleepwalking? I don't know. But I headed back upstairs and tried to get back to sleep.

This time I was actually able to sleep without any weird dreams or having strange feelings. It was some of the best sleep I have had in a while.

The next morning the movers had arrived and we got the house in order. I told dad about the conversation with Logan. He was very pleased that I stood up for myself and that I had broken things off with him. Dad never liked him and if Logan were to show up here now...well that would not be a pretty sight.

Logan showed up at Alex's banging on the door. Furious, face red, eyes welled. "Alex open up! I need to talk to you!" He yelled.

Alex opened the door, "Yo Brooks! You are back already? Why...oh wait you heard about Jay's move."

"What! You knew? Why the hell didn't you tell me!" He demanded.

"Look Brooks, we found out, well, Nikki found out the night we got back from the lake. We didn't say anything to you about it because of how you treated her and made her feel, and honestly it showed when we were at the lake and you basically told her she couldn't swim or you were not taking her home. Common dude! Wake-up call! She doesn't want to be treated like that! She doesn't deserve it! Dude you never treat a woman like that! Show some respect man!" Alex told him in a stern tone.

"So, you knew about this, you knew about her move? You son of a bitch!"

Logan grabbed Alex by the collar of his shirt and slammed him up against the wall, giving Alex the most furious look.

"You ever betray me like that again, you will regret it! You will work on getting her back here with me where she belongs!" Logan screamed at him and punched Alex in the face knocking him down.

Logan started to walk out the door. Alex got up and noticed his nose was bleeding. He ran up behind Logan and pushed him; Logan stumbled and caught himself before falling. Logan came back up, turning towards Alex, and went for another swing. Alex ducked and got a few punches into Logan's stomach and one to the face. He then managed to get Logan in a headlock. Logan was trying to break free and jabbed Alex in the ribs with his elbow. Alex took the blow to the ribs and took Logan all the way to the ground, pinning him with no way to break free.

"See, this is why I won the state championship in wrestling when we were in school. Think I've forgotten it? Guess again, bro! Go on, try to break free; you know damn well you won't be able to. Now, Logan, you are gonna listen whether you like it or not! You know I will kick your ass, so don't try anything like that again! You need a wake-up call, bro, and I'm the one who is gonna give it to ya. You need it, and you need it now!"

"Look, Alex, I don't need your lil pep talk or whatever you want to call it. I know what I am doing and what I want! Now let me the hell up!"

"Bro, I'll let you up, but you best listen and listen good. Got it?"

"Fine, I'll listen!" He grunted, "Just let me up already!"

Alex let him up. They had a few beers and a long conversation about his attitude and how he treated Jaycenda, and how much she had been miserable and could not take it anymore. For the first time in Logan's life, he began to show that he actually cared about someone else other than himself and began to cry.

"I just never realized I was hurting her," he said as tears streamed down his face. "I love her, I screwed up majorly. How can I ever fix what I had done to her?" He asked as he looked toward Alex for guidance.

"First of all, you need to apologize to her if you want to try to make things right between you. If you truly love her and want to marry her, bro, you better damn well start treating her with respect and show her how much you truly care about her, if that's what you want. But also remember I am also her friend, and if you do work things out, the minute you start disrespecting her again, you are going to have to deal with me!" Alex told him.

"I understand, and yes, I want her back in my arms. Hell, I am willing to work on things even if it would be long distance. Alex, I don't want to lose her! I love her too damn much!"

"Alright, Brooks, I will try to help. Whatever her decision is, let it be. If she chooses not to try to work it out, you need to respect that. Do not push her. I will do the calling and talk to her first. K?"

"Alright, man, thanks, bro," he said as they hit their fists together.

Ring, ring, ring…

"Hello."

"Hey, Jay! It's Alex."

"Hey, stranger! How are you and Nikki? I miss you guys sooo much!"

"We miss you too, Jay! It's good to hear your voice. Hey, um, I have someone here who wants to talk to you. Please just listen."

"Alex, no! I'm not ready!"

"Please, Jay, just listen. That's all I ask, what you choose to do, you know Nikki and I support you one hundred percent."

"Fine," I said in an unpleasant tone.

"Jay, it's me, Logan. Look, I know that the last thing you want to do is talk to me. Please hear me out. Alex and I had a heart-to-heart, and I never realized I was hurting you. I never realized how you felt. I am so sorry, Jay! I love you, and I am so sorry!" Logan began to sob, "I never meant to hurt you, I miss you, Jay, please forgive me and give me another chance to prove it. I will make it right!" He pleaded.

I began to wonder if what Logan was saying was true, if I should give him another chance. He was, after all, actually crying, or so it seemed, and Logan Brooks never cries at anything.

"Logan, I don't know if I can. You had always disrespected me and treated me like crap. I do love you, but I don't think you will be able to change your ways. Besides that, I am in North Carolina now and there is no way it could ever work out," I told him.

"Baby, I love you and miss you! We can make this work! I want nothing more than that! I swear I will change! I want you to be happy and I want to be that guy who makes you happy. I am willing to work on it even though it is long distance. Baby, I will visit every other weekend, and from time to time, I will even bring Nikki and Alex down. Please, Jay, give me another chance," he pleaded once again.

The whole baby thing was new, and it did feel kinda nice; it was much better than the whole "you are my goddess" crap.

"One more chance, Logan, and that is it. If you start to go back to the way it was before, it is definitely over. I do not deserve it, and I will not tolerate it like I had before," I said.

We had talked some more. He did seem to have changed, and the fact he had cried had gotten my attention that he had been serious about everything. It was amazing how different he had seemed to be. Dad and I had talked about the conversation. Dad really did not want to see me go back to him but was willing to be nice whenever Logan came to visit. Still, he made it very clear he was not to sleep in my room or in the guest room. He was to be downstairs on the couch. I don't think Logan would mind as long as he was here with me.

Chapter 4

The next morning, I got up bright and early, having enjoyed a good night's sleep with no disturbances or bad dreams. I got dressed and went downstairs. It looked like Dad was getting ready to try his hand at cooking again. He looked up at me and asked if I wanted to take over. I laughed and told him absolutely. He did manage to make some great coffee, which would be kind of hard to mess up.

After breakfast, Dad and I went to explore the property. Dad armed himself with his rifle and knife. He stated he was not going to go walk in the woods without protection, considering we were in the mountains. He did not want to take any chances running into any bears or mountain lions. It was a nice opportunity to spend quality time with Dad, something we hadn't had much of since arriving. We came upon a stream, and I told Dad I needed to take a breather. I started to have the feeling of burning all over and then going to freezing. In a split second, everything went black, and the next thing I knew, I was further up the stream from Dad.

"Jay, don't move!" Dad yelled, raising his rifle.

At the same time I felt something behind me, turning around to find a black bear just a few feet away on its hind legs, growling loudly. Scared yet angry, I instinctively put my arms up and pushed them towards the bear. Out of nowhere, the bear was lifted off the ground and thrown back into a tree about twenty feet away. You could hear how hard the bear had hit it. It got back up and looked over at me and then limped away.

Dad came running up and hugged me.

"Are you okay, sweetie?"

"Yeah, Dad, I'm okay, but what was that? I didn't touch the bear or anything."

"Well, I think you just started tapping into some of your powers your mother mentioned. It is probably best if we head back to the house."

"I think that would be good; I do feel a little weak after that."

Back at the house, I went up to my room to lay down, pondering what was happening to me. Why couldn't I just be normal? No half-Atlantean, no special powers, no visions. I wished for answers, and also for normalcy.

That night, I had a pleasant dream. I dreamt of a man with beautiful green eyes, a captivating smile, thick kissable lips, and short hair that he spiked up, and somewhat of a square jaw line. I could only see him from the shoulders up. The way he looked at me, gave me the butterflies; he was so beautiful; he literally took my breath away. He looked over his should and nodded. He gestured towards a window, and as I looked out, we were swiftly approaching a circular wall—it must be Atlantis.

The city looked huge, there had been three motes, surrounding the city, making it look like a circular island between each mote and in the middle on top of a hill that appeared to be a palace that was a cross between Egyptian and Greek architecture, the city's entirety looked to be more of Greek architecture. It was merely a glimpse, as he and the city faded, and I woke up, unable to identify the man but there was something about him I cannot describe. Maybe he was just a figment of my imagination, but he was the most gorgeous man I had ever seen.

In some way, I was hoping he was real. I know that it is wrong of me to say considering I am now back with Logan. What was I thinking? It was a dream and only a dream.

I could not fall back sleep, so I got ready, made coffee, and watched the sunrise on the porch. The dream lingered; there was something about him that made me smile. If only he were real, though I knew it was just a dream.

Dad wanted me to meet his friend Trish. We went into town, and I drove the new truck. We met at the diner, its front with filled with various flowers and bushes, creating an arbor filled with ivy into a covered porch built around a willow tree. There were several tables on the porch. In the corner by the fountain sat a woman, Trish, with shoulder-length brown hair looking at a menu. She looked up smiled and waved at dad. Dad smiled back and walked over to her. He introduced us. She seemed nice. I found it funny that she was flirting with dad and he did not seem to notice.

We had lunch and talked a good bit. Trish mentioned it was nice to have new faces in town and continued smiling at Dad. After we chatted Dad and I walked around the town square and went to explore some of the shops. I loved how the town was surrounded by the mountains. We spent a few hours in town and then headed home.

Chapter 5

Milledge made his way back to his chambers after taking the queen her breakfast. He had gone to his sleeping chamber and laid down on the feathered mattress, arms stretched out, and hands behind his head, staring at the ceiling, thinking of what things will be like when he tries to overtake Atlantis when it has risen.

He had a few followers, not many to overtake. His solution he and Dylian came up with: they had created a few of a specific creature they called the Nibus. Dylian was the genetic engineer; Milledge was the mastermind behind the creature. Still growing, the Nibus were the only things that Milledge was so proud of; they were his babies in a sense.

He had a secret chamber within his chamber that he and Dylian would work on their creature. It was also where he held Enid. His Aunt Millicent, who was the only mystic and had an apprentice following in her footsteps. She had placed an enchantment on Milledge's chamber as well as on both him and Dylian so the Seers would not pick up on their doings.

Millicent had been on Milledge's side up to a certain extent. She didn't always agree with him, but he was family, and that to her was enough to protect him. She owned the Gallo, one of the few pubs in the market. She had placed protection on it, as Milledge and Dylian would gather there in a secret room from time to time, without looking suspicious.

Milledge wanted Millicent to commit fully to what he was doing as her powers were great. Her apprentice Bray was still learning much; he would be no use to him.

He needed to go to his sanctuary and needed to take care of Enid. He was trying too hard to get her to reveal everything she had seen prior to keeping her captive. He knew with the enchantment Millicent had on his chambers she may never have had or will have any visions. She was feisty not telling him anything over the years he had held her captive. Enough with the games, his caring for her was done. It was time to try an invention he recently finished creating to try to get her to talk.

He got up and walked over to the far side of the room. He had pushed in the carved head of a bull; part of the wall had opened up. When he got to the second step, he reached to his right and twisted another carved head of a bull, and the wall closed behind him. He continued down the spiral stone staircase, the crystals being his light source. When he got to the bottom of the stairs, he looked around in amazement that this hidden chamber no one but he and Dylian knew about other than his family. This chamber had always been in his family, much like everyone else's residency for the most part of Atlantis.

He went straight ahead to the far wall where he had a small

rectangular table and one chair. He sat down and waved his hand in the air. A clear screen appeared out of nowhere with some of his writings already on the screen. He took the oblong crystal that was pointed at the end and began to write. He had changed the screen to check on his species and Dylian created, checking on their growth in what he and Dylian named the breeding dome. He made a few notes and waved his hand, and the screen disappeared. Milledge created many things mainly mechanical. This was the first time he had actually created something living, with Dylian's help as he is one of the head genetic engineers for Atlantis.

He walked over to a small bush he was growing and picked the unusual berries from it. They were small and orange in color, and very sweet. He fed these to Enid most of the time, as just a few of them were filling. Some days he would be generous and bring her full meals. He walked toward the red curtain and went behind it, leading to another room. Enid was lying on a metallic table with crystal restraints over her wrists and ankles. He went over and fed her the berries. He did let her up three times a day to bathe and what not.

"My dear Enid, how are you today?"

"How do you think I am?!? I am being held against my will, and by the one whom I had trusted rand once loved!"

"My dear Enid, you know what I want. I want you to tell me

of the visions you have had. You never do tell. You would not be restrained if you were to tell me. I kept you around Enid; I could have killed you like I did with Baron and Darmel. But you are here. I care for you Enid, but I grow weary of you keeping what I want to know away from me. You are very beautiful, your long dark brown hair, beautiful smile, which reminds me, I have not seen that smile in such a long time. Shame really. I would love to see that smile again."

"Unbelievable Milledge! Why would I want to smile for you again?"

"Enid, you need to tell me. I cannot stress this enough. Tell me everything. If you do not comply, I will have no choice but to do things to you I do not want to do. Time is short." He said as he leaned over her looking straight into her eyes.

"You see Enid, December is not too far off. Only six months away. I want to know what you have seen. It is of importance."

"Yes, Milledge, I have. Your ancestor Cyrus wanted complete control over the world, and you want to fulfill what he could not. You do not want peace and harmony with the humans. I will not tell you what I have seen. I don't care if you keep me held like this or if you kill me. There is still time for you, Milledge, to stop dwelling on this and realize the world needs peace and harmony. I know you thrive on the wars that happen above, but ask yourself, is it all worth it? Once the alignment takes place, much of the world will be destroyed. Why would you want to do this? Why are you so adamant about ruling Atlantis and the world? What do you have to gain from it?"

"Enid, Enid, tsk, tsk. I am royal by blood; it is my right. Cyrus should never have been killed. I should be the one who has access to the throne and the labyrinth; I want all the knowledge; I want it all. I know if I were to enter the labyrinth, I would be killed. I need access to that labyrinth; I need to know how the outcome will be, Enid. Even if the majority of the world will be destroyed, I want the control; I must have the control. Atlantis and the world only need one ruler - ME! I need to know what I need to achieve, Enid. This would be a new beginning; the humans would be our servants and obey every order given to them. I do not understand why you do not see things my way. I want what is rightfully mine. Enid, please, what have you seen?"

"I will never say, Milledge!" She screamed at him and spat in his face.

Milledge wiped his face.

"You want to play games, do you?"

Milledge went over to the room on his right. He came back with a metallic headband. Inside the headband were small metallic beads surrounding the circular headband with small sharp triangular crystals sticking out of each one.

"Enid, I am probably one of the most intelligent Atlanteans. I should not be a servant, period. I have so many creative things and now more or less new creations. I believe you know I enjoy my little experiments. This is something I have been working on for some time now. Enid, you will tell me what I need to know willingly, or I will place this on you, and you will endure great pain, and you will want to tell me. Either way, the choice is yours."

"Milledge, I will not tell you, even if you place that upon me. If it hurts me, I will deal with the pain. I shall not tell you anything."

"Enid, I do not think you understand. When I place this on you, you will be in great pain. This little genius device I created will make you tell me."

Enid looked at him in disbelief. This man she once had feelings for was doing this to her. She had once missed running her fingers through his long curly hair when they had spent the night together. She had once missed looking into his dark brown eyes. She wanted the old Milledge back, who cared about her. Not this evil person who was bound to have whatever he wanted.

Milledge placed the band on her head. Enid started to feel the pain. Tears were streaming down her face. She was thinking she would be able to tolerate the pain, but the pain began to worsen. She felt as though someone was squeezing her head harder and harder.

She began to scream in agony.

"The true heir!" She screamed aloud.

Milledge took the band off.

"Now, Enid, do you want to tell me everything without the band on?" He asked.

She was still in pain and sobbing.

"Without, Milledge. The pain is too much; I cannot bear it." She said in a low voice still sobbing.

"Let me make things a bit more comfortable for you." He said to her looking into her eyes.

He lifted the crystal restraints from her wrists and ankles and helped her up. She had been too weak to stand. He picked her up and carried her to the room off to the left. There in the room was a feathered mattress and pillow on the floor and the room off from it was the bathing room. She often wondered why he never held her in here instead of that horrible table with the restraints. He laid her down on the mattress.

"Milledge, please, why do you do this?" She asked in a weak tone.

"You came to me questioning about why I wanted to take over. I could not allow you to go to Helena or any of the other royals about it. Baron and Darmel, well, I had to well… I had to dispose of them. I could not do that to you, Enid. We were once lovers; we once cared for one another. I could not harm you, but I had to make sure over the past few years you, you wouldn't say anything. I wanted to know what you had seen. Besides, I would rather keep a beautiful woman around than another man." He laughed.

"Now tell me before I start to get angry, Enid, I do not wish to harm you again. Time is running out. What visions have you had?" He asked one last time.

Enid was lying on the mattress; she was the weakest she had ever been in her lifetime. She looked up at him, not wanting to believe the man she once loved so long ago was keeping her prisoner.

"Milledge, before I say anything, I have to say this. I once had feelings for you. You doing what you have done to me made me hate you. I cannot bear the pain of that device you had placed on my head. So I will tell you what I had visions of. Keep in mind we seers only see glimpses and may not have foreseen everything you want to know."

"Enid, I do care for you, but do not hate me. Understand why I had to do what I did. You know I want my rightful place on the throne. Tell me what I need to know."

"Fine, Luciana had a child. I do not know her name; however, she bears a mark. From what I have seen, rather from my understanding of a vision, she is the true heir to the throne, ruler of Atlantis. This I do not understand, nor can I explain. I saw you befriend her, whether a true friendship or not, I do not know. Although at this point, I would say not. What your intentions are with her, I do not have the answer you may seek."

Milledge interrupted, "Wait, Luciana had a child? She bears the mark? When did this occur?"

"Yes, when she was among the humans. She had the child."

"Interesting… go on."

"Your heart has blackened, Milledge. It blackens more each day."

"Now, now, beautiful, let's not get ahead of ourselves. Continue on with the visions."

"Milledge, you also fall in love with a human. I see she has a good heart. But you will be quick to manipulate her into your antics. That is all I have seen."

"Do not lie to me. That would not be a good thing."

"I came to you asking you about it because I saw what you wanted to do. If you want to know if you succeed or not, I do not have that answer; I never saw anything more than what I had asked you. You know we do not get visions all the time, Milledge. They come when they come. You can go a whole year without having a vision. Do you want me to lie and give you false information?”

“I suppose you are right. However, this falling in love with a human? Please, I have not any interest.”

“Milledge, please, if you do care for me at all, please do not restrain me again.”

“Alright, I will grant you your request. I will allow you to remain in this room where it will be more comfortable for you.” He responded.

“I prefer if you just release me. I will not say anything about this, Milledge. I will just tell the royals I went above for the last three years.”

“You know I cannot do that. I cannot take that chance.” He told her as he left the room, locking the door behind him.

Enid already knew her fate; all she wanted was to see her family and friends one last time.

Chapter 6

Helena and Luciana were sitting across from each other in Helena's chamber, both in awe of the history they had learned from the crystal.

"Now that we have learned a good bit of history that we have not known about, we need to have a meeting with the other royals. I will summon Milledge to gather the others into the Great Hall," Helena stated.

Helena walked over to the granite table near the doorway and waved her hand, summoning a screen.

"Milledge," she said into the screen.

His face appeared on the screen.

"Yes, Your Majesty," he said.

"Milledge, I need for you to gather the royals for a meeting in the Great Hall. Please have a pitcher of wine and cheese ready for when everyone arrives. We will meet in one hour."

"Yes, Your Majesty," he stated. When Helena waved her hand, the screen disappeared.

"Now, Luciana, we must prepare. After the meeting, I will allow you to go see Jaycenda, however, I will need you back in two days' time."

"Oh, thank you, Helena!" Luciana said with a big smile as she hugged Helena, her eyes welling up.

"Luciana, you need to see her. You had kept this secret for such a long time. I could not imagine if I had to spend twenty years not seeing Kyrie. She may come back with you if she chooses. It will be her decision to stay here until we rise or stay with her father until the time comes."

"Helena, I cannot thank you enough!"

"She bears the mark, Luciana. One thing we have learned, surprisingly, is that her power may be far greater than that of a Mystic. Although the crystal had not specified that, it is merely a guess."

"Yes, she has much to learn," Luciana stated.

"Come now, we must make our way to the Great Hall."

"Yes, Helena."

Helena and Luciana left for the Great Hall, passing through several corridors and ascending the marble staircase. At the top of the stairs, the doorway to the room of the thrones awaited them. They entered the room, with its red marble floor, a circular design with unusual etchings in the middle of the floor, and gold-trimmed pillars. On the left, three large windows overlooked the courtyard, their dark blue draperies closed. A golden chandelier hung from the ceiling, illuminating the spacious room. To the right of the throne room, they entered the doorway to the Great Hall, furnished with an oblong black granite table, crimson-colored marbled floor, and off-white draperies. Eight chairs surrounded the table, the tallest on each end trimmed in gold.

Helena took her seat at the very end of the table, Luciana and Kyrie sitting beside her. Marcade and Recil took their places across from Kyrie and Luciana.

"As you know, I have called upon this meeting of high importance," Helena stated. Everyone nodded.

"Asher and Airleen had a vision in which I needed to speak with Luciana, which is why she is here. Luciana, please fill them in."

"Thank you, Your Majesty."

"Luciana, we are all on a first-name basis here in this meeting. Do not feel the need to call any of us Majesty," Helena stated.

"Yes, Helena, thank you. As you know, many years ago, I spent two years above. I had fallen in love and had given birth to a daughter. Her name is Jaycenda. She bears the mark of the intertwined half-moons on her left shoulder."

Helena interrupted, "Which means she is the true heir to the throne, the true High Queen. Continue, Luciana."

"She is half Atlantean, half human. I had a vision of some of her powers. I do not know if she has tapped into any of her powers; however, I have no idea how great or how small her powers are." Luciana stated.

Helena then spoke, "I know this is against the rules; however, she bears the mark that we cannot deny. I am not going to punish Luciana. In fact, I am allowing her to visit with her daughter for two days and giving her the option to return here with Luciana before the events. Kyrie, my son, you will accompany Luciana and assist Jaycenda, teach her what we Atlanteans are about, help her learn her history."

"Yes, Mother," Kyrie responded.

"Now furthermore, Luciana and I had gone into the labyrinth and recovered little information as we are short on time. We knew very little about those who bear the 'mark' and, we know little about our ancestry before Atlantis went under. We must give the upmost respect to the one who bears the mark. As they are the true heir to the throne, and they have powers that may even be greater than the mystics. We need to prepare her as she will be the new High Queen. She will need to learn our way of life," Helena stated.

"If you will no longer be Queen, and I no longer the main heir to the throne, then who shall replace her should something happen to her?" Kyrie asked.

"I would go back to being the High Queen and in following suite as before Kyrie. You, Recil, and then Marcade."

"I see. When shall I accompany Luciana?"

"Today. You have not yet been above. I would like for you to have the chance to go above and have that experience before the events. You have only seen it visually when you were learning to be a watcher in the tower with Daj."

"Thank you, Mother, for this opportunity."

"Anyone have questions?" Helena asked.

Marcade spoke. "What exactly have you learned from the crystal besides the one who bears the mark? You mentioned you learned more of our ancestry but have yet to speak of it."

"We only know of our history dating back to when Atlantis had gone under and how we kept our civilization secret. We would keep watch on the humans and their developments. What we had learned that we have no prior knowledge of until now is that we have descended here to Earth from Mars. That had been our home. When our ancestors learned a meteor was to hit and destroy us, we made Earth our new home."

"When we had arrived here on Earth there was another race, a reptilian race—the Anunnaki. We assisted them with the humans to advance starting with the Sumerians. The Anunnaki knew we were already advanced and needing to make a new home on Earth."

"For many years we worked with the Anunnaki helping the human race to advance. We had even made a pact to continue to watch over the humans and to make sure they do not get too far advanced beyond our races. The Anunnaki had left Earth to return to their home planet while we kept watch. They had left Atlantis to us leaving their knowledge along with ours."

"Both races had our own language, but we were able to understand each other somehow. We no longer have knowledge of the language our race had once spoken. All we knew was that Arcadian had come forth with the mark and had sunk Atlantis."

"Now that we know those who bear the mark have great powers can do so much more. He also felt the world needed cleansing and had somehow with his powers had all the Atlanteans and humans forget the past. Forget where we originated from, the pact we had with the Anunnaki. Forget how structures were built."

"We assisted the Mayans and gave them knowledge and gave them access to the prophecies as to what is to come; to keep a record for those to prepare for the events. We helped many cultures advance and develop and create structures that still stand today. Many, who think it will be the end, will indeed be a new beginning. There will be massive destruction, this world needs cleansing. We will be assisting the survivors, help them rebuild a new life. Things will be different than what those above will be used to."

"Once we have risen, the dome shall remain until it is safe from the destruction to have the dome come undone. Jaycenda is the only one who will be able to undo the dome. From what Luciana had foreseen, there will be thick ash that will be blocking the sun, for how long is uncertain. The great pyramid will still be standing, mostly covered in sand."

"According to one of Luciana's visions Jaycenda will need to enter the pyramid; she will have the power to make some changes with the Earth. We are not exactly sure how this will work; it is only what Luciana had foreseen."

"That is all we have had time to learn from the crystal. Luciana, Kyrie; go pack and be at the third tier in one hour," Helena told them.

They nodded and went to their separate chambers to pack some clothing. Luciana and Kyrie met at the Great Entrance of the palace.

"Are you ready?" Kyrie asked.

"Very much so! I have missed my daughter and Sam more than anyone could know, Kyrie!"

Kyrie smiled at her.

They walked down the cobble-stoned path aligned with columns and arched stonework. When they reached the edge, there was a very long steep staircase leading down to an arched bridge. They walked over to the right side of the staircase. There was a glowing platform that stuck out over the edge.

They both stepped onto the platform and put their shoulder bags down. They were overlooking a majority of Atlantis, vast in its size. Looking down, they could see the third mote and the third tier filled with the market, the garden of Artillia, and the Coliseum.

Beyond that, the second tier was filled with residencies, and then the first tier consisting of the agriculture and farmland, and the great wall. A hand railing rose up on the platform. They placed their hands on the railing. The platform started to descend. Luciana looked to her left while descending, looking at the long marbled staircase to the marbled arched bridge with the carved stone railings on the staircase and bridge.

The platform stopped a few feet above the water and turned right, continuing around the mote with the water creating small, rippled waves as they continued on. They continued around the palace. As they came around the bend, they saw a large stone structure beside a fleet of airships. At the end of the building, the platform made a left turn and made its way to the bank at the end of the structure. There was one step up to the ground level. Once the platform interlocked in front of the step, the railings went down into the platform. They grabbed their bags and placed them over their shoulder and went up the step. Daj came out of the building wearing a one-piece dark suit.

"My lady Luciana, I was told to be expecting you and Prince Kyrie," he said.

"Yes, Daj, is the ship ready?" Luciana asked.

"Yes, follow me."

"I do get to test my ability to fly the ship, correct?" Kyrie asked Luciana.

Luciana laughed. "Kyrie, it flies on its own. You just put in the coordinates, sit back, and enjoy the views," she said.

"I see," he said, disappointed.

They followed Daj down the first row of ships. They had seen one of the ships coming into the dome and land. There were many different ships of shapes and sizes. They came to the end of the row.

"Here we are. This is the ship you will be taking," he said.

The ship was triangular and stretched out about twenty feet long. Both Luciana and Kyrie thanked Daj as he started to leave them and head back to the structure. Luciana placed her hand on the bottom of the ship; underneath the ship, a bright light appeared.

They walked into the light and were quickly taken up in the ship. There was a total of six seats on the ship.

Luciana and Kyrie took the first two seats in front of the window. Luciana waved her hand, and a screen appeared with bright blue numbers and lettering. She put in the coordinates and waved her hand for the screen to disappear. She smiled at Kyrie. "Off we go."

Chapter 7

Kyrie was very excited to be going above for the first time. He clapped his hands and rubbed them together. "Finally!" he said in excitement.

The ship rose above the other ships and started to pick up speed quickly, shooting out of the dome into blackness. Soon, they passed a school of dolphins, and Kyrie was amazed at all the different sea life they were encountering, even though it was a mere glimpse. He was grateful to have this experience, as he had only seen these creatures when he filled in for a watcher at times.

"Will the humans detect us?" he asked.

"No, Kyrie. We are in a stealth cloaking; no one or anything will detect us. It cannot be seen unless we wish it to be seen. We will be reaching land very soon; we will be there shortly. The speed of this ship will get us there in no time."

"Good. This is amazing. I am looking forward to meeting your daughter and her father," he said.

"I am looking forward to introducing you. I have been waiting to see them again for such a long time. It has seemed like what the humans call… an eternity."

They had arrived at their destination. It was mid-morning; the ship hovered above the driveway. They left the ship and proceeded onto the porch, knocking on the door.

"Dad, someone is knocking on the door, could you get that?" I asked while I was unloading the dishwasher.

"Huh, I didn't hear anyone knocking, wasn't expecting anyone," he said as he placed the bottled water in the refrigerator.

Dad answered the door. "Oh my! I… I… can't believe it!" he yelled in astonishment. "Jay, get in here now!"

I ran into the living room; Dad was at the door hugging a woman and giving her several quick kisses. She looked over at me with tears in her eyes, smiling. It was my mother. Dad stepped aside, and she came running over to me, giving me a very long hug. I closed my eyes, crying and smiling; I couldn't believe she was finally here.

"I love you so much! Please forgive me for leaving you when you were only a few weeks along. I had to return home and could not take you with me. I have waited all this time to see you," she said in excitement. I could feel her tears drip onto my shirt.

"It's okay, Mom. I have been waiting for this moment also!"

As I opened my eyes while still hugging my mother, there he was, the man from my dream! He looked exactly like I had dreamt, the spiky brown hair, almond-shaped green eyes, every detail. He was standing beside my dad. My heart was pounding so hard; he looked at me and gave me a wink and a smile. I had never felt like my knees would ever give out until now. I felt as though I could not breathe; I could not believe he was real. My heart sunk. Nikki was right, when you know who you are meant to be with, you just know. I had this feeling come all over me that I have never felt before, very intense; words really cannot describe this feeling. I let go of my mother and walked over toward him.

"H-hi, I'm Jaycenda," I said nervously.

"Hello Jaycenda, pleased to meet you. I am Kyrie," he stated with a smile and another wink.

My heart just melted. I went to shake his hand; he gently grabbed my hand and kissed it. I am sure he noticed my blushing and shaking. I could not help it.

We all sat down and talked about our lives. I was amazed to find out that Kyrie was actually a Prince. Huh, who would have known, he sure looks it. I could not stop looking into his eyes, listening to his deep voice, loving how he would look at me like no other has ever looked at me.

I never would have imagined this moment seeing my mother finally and then the man from my dream. I tried not constantly to look at him although it was hard not to. He was very much real, not a figment of my imagination.

My phone rang. I just let it ring. I did not care who it was, whether it was Nikki, Alex, or even Logan. This moment I wanted to always remember without any interruptions. The phone would stop after several rings then go back to ringing again. I finally shut the phone off after the third time.

Later that evening, Dad wanted to show Mom around town and offered for Kyrie and me to tag along. I did not want to go. I couldn't; I just wanted to be here with Kyrie. Kyrie stated he would stay behind with me.

Dad and Mom had left. I showed Kyrie around, and we opened up more about ourselves. I asked him if he minded if I called him Ky instead. He said he liked that very much and did not mind at all, and would prefer to be called Ky.

After I showed Ky the house, I then showed him the area Dad had built into the mountain.

I had this unbelievable feeling come all over me; it felt as though I can honestly say I was in love, true love at that, for the first time in my life, and at first sight. It was like a burst of energy running throughout my body. We went to the room off to the left and sat down on the couch. I sat at one end; he sat on the other end. We talked, and we both smiled at each other. I had to look away a few times from being so nervous. Being around him I felt complete, my heart was whole. I have never had this with Logan or anyone.

"Can I ask you a question?" he asked.

"Sure, ask away," I said, all giddy.

"Can I kiss you?" he asked.

I know I was blushing; I could not believe this gorgeous man that you could say I fell for before we actually met—I guess you could say love at first sight—had just asked to kiss me. Was I dreaming again? If so, I surely do not want to wake up!

"Yes, you can," I said with a huge smile on my face.

"Come over here," he said.

"How about we meet in the middle?" I asked.

We scooted to the middle of the couch. We both looked into each other's eyes, smiling. I was so nervous. He took his hand and cupped my face. I loved feeling his touch. It felt so right. His touch was compassionate and irresistible. He moved in closer. He closed his eyes, and I had closed mine. He had kissed me softly. I did not want to stop. I had never been so overwhelmed with happiness and the feeling that Ky was giving me; I did not want it to end. I knew he was the one, even before we had met. Ky made me feel safe and well, loved in a sense.

We continued kissing; it seemed like a forever bliss. I could not help myself; I could not hold back, neither could Ky. We let ourselves get lost in the moment, and we made love. It was beautiful, and we just laid there afterward in each other's arms for a little while. Yes, I can honestly say I am in love. I now know what Nikki was talking about. And I could not stop smiling.

We got our clothes back on. As we proceeded to leave the room, he grabbed my hand and pulled me over to him, giving me a long hug and another kiss. Smiling at each other, and then we left and went upstairs into the living room; he continued to hold my hand. I turned on the television. He was laying on the couch and motioned for me to join him. I laid on the couch, my back facing his stomach and my head resting right below his neck. He wrapped his arms around me holding me tightly. I loved this feeling and did not want it to end. I have never been so happy.

Mom and Dad soon came home laughing as they entered, holding hands. They looked over at Kyrie and me and had a stunned look on their faces.

"Hi Dad, Mom," I said with a smile.

"Well uh, hello, you two," she said.

"Kyrie, what exactly is going on with you and my daughter?" Mom asked with an odd look on her face. Dad looked like he was happy with it. We both looked at each other, smiling.

"Jaycenda has started to call me Ky, short for Kyrie, which I prefer to go by from now on. I do not know what it is about

Jaycenda. She makes me feel complete, I have to say she and I both feel whole and happy with each other. I plan to be with her."

Mom about fainted. Dad was shocked but yet seemed happy about it, I mean after all look how Logan had treated me. Crap! Yeah, I definitely am ending it whether he likes it or not. I have a choice, and my choice is for happiness and true love.

Dad finally spoke. "I know you are a prince and all, but my daughter? I do not know you all that well. I don't like the thought of Jay being with anyone."

"And Ky, you are already betrothed to marry," Mother stated, and this deeply disappointed me as I was not expecting this news.

"I know Luciana and I am calling it off. I cannot explain it, nor do I want to try to explain it, however, Jaycenda is whom I wish to be with."

At this moment I was giddy, I was happy. He is choosing to be with me.

"Well Jay, what are you going to do about Logan? After all, you seem to be in the same situation as Ky," Dad reminded me.

"Dad, for the record, I really did not want to marry Logan. I was ready to break things off, and he pulled the ring out and slipped it on then left to go on vacation with his parents, and we moved down here. I know I put up a fight about it, but I did not want to leave Nikki and Alex behind.”

“Humph. Well, I am perfectly fine with Ky, I hated Logan, uh no offense. Luciana? Your thoughts?” Dad asked.

“I, well, I am at a loss for words, honestly.”

“Well, this has been a great day, I think we should all get some sleep,” Dad said while pretending to yawn. He and Mom started to walk up the stairs; Ky and I followed. Dad turned around and looked Ky in the eye. “Oh, by the way Ky, prince, or no prince, you are not going to share my daughter’s bed. You can take the couch.” Nodding his head toward downstairs.

“But Dad! I am an adult!”

“And I am your father, and this is my house.”

“Well, what about the third bedroom?”

“That is too close to your room, don’t think so. Not gonna happen. I hear everything, even in a deep sleep, so Ky, do not try to sneak up here.”

“Yes, sir,” Ky responded surprised that someone actually told him what he can and cannot do, this was a first for him, he will respect Sam’s wishes. After all, Sam is approving of he and Jaycenda being together.

Ky grabbed me and gave me a long hug and kissed me softly

and wished me a nice good night; he looked into my eyes smiling, then turned around and went downstairs.

I turned around and proceeded up to the top of the stairs; mom was waiting in front of my door, dad standing behind her. She hugged me and told me how much she loved me, and I told her how much I loved her and was so thankful she came to us and brought Ky with her.

She let go and smiled, dad wished me a good night. They proceeded down the hall to dad's room. Yeah, I don't even want to think about what they may be up to tonight.

I closed my door and got ready for bed. I laid down smiling remembering what Ky and I had done earlier. I couldn't resist. There was something about him, and he made me feel special. He had never given me attitude; he didn't force me into anything I didn't want to do. It felt so right. I fell asleep happy for once.

I woke up feeling like I was on fire again. Looking at the ceiling, I couldn't scream, I couldn't move. I don't know how long I had been asleep for until this happened. I felt paralyzed, having a hard time breathing. I did not understand any of this.

Mom came bursting into my room, yelling for Dad and Ky and yelling for me to look at her, trying to shake me. Suddenly I snapped out of it.

"Jaycenda, baby!" Mom sobbed and felt relieved as she grabbed me, hugging me. Dad and Ky came rushing into my room questioning what was going on.

"I, uh, dunno. I was having a bad dream or vision, whatever you want to call it. I woke up not able to speak or move, feeling like I was on fire."

I told them about the dream. Another one of destruction, many wildfires, cities falling into lava, balls of fire in the sky, cities being flooded. At one point seeing a city in the middle between being flooded and lava striking it, seeing people both drowning and being burned alive in the lava. Watching this hindering sight; of water and lava overcoming a city merging. Words cannot describe this awful deadly sight I was seeing. Tornados ripping through cities. At times several touching down at the same time. There was nothing I could do but watch and feel saddened.

"Jaycenda, sweetie," Mom said in a soothing tone. "It was not a dream; it was a vision of the future."

"I don't want this," I said shaking my head. "I don't want this. Why don't we just go ahead and save people before this is to come instead of all this horrible destruction and death?" I asked.

"We cannot save everyone. This world needs cleansing. There will be survivors; there is room for many. We can only do so much. The warnings have already been in place for a very long time;

those who choose to heed those warnings will know how to survive. Those who brush it off will meet their end. However, there are those who may have been preparing but not able to avoid what is to come."

"I also have visions. We are both seers. You cannot control it. They come when they come. You need to talk about them. You have them more so than I. What you have seen is what is to be; it is out of your control. This is only part of your destiny, Jaycenda. I need for you to come back to Atlantis with Ky and me; when it is time, I will come back for you, Sam."

"I cannot be there for that long away from Dad. Can't I just go and visit for a few days and come back here until it's time for you to come back to us?"

"I am afraid not."

"I have to think about it long and hard. Dad has always been there for me when I needed him; I don't know if I could be away from dad for so long, even if just for a few months. I can talk to him about anything; he is my rock."

"I know sweetie. Please think about it."

"I will," I said as I gave mom a long hug. "How did you know to come to me?"

"I knew," she said with a smile.

I looked over at the doorway. Ky was standing there smiling;

the moonlight was shining into my room; he looks so handsome standing there. He came over to hug me and give me a kiss and let me know everything is going to be alright. It did not matter what dad had said, he stayed with me the rest of the night holding me, making sure I was going to be fine. I had felt so safe in his arms.

The next morning, we went out for breakfast. I didn't feel like cooking, and dad, well, he can be dangerous in the kitchen. I was not going to allow him to attempt it. The mountains were beautiful, but on the way back I had to pull over and let dad drive. I was getting sick with all the twists and turns in the roads, and with the visions coming and going I didn't want to risk crashing all of us.

We arrived back at the cabin. Dad wanted to talk to Ky privately, and mom and I wanted to have some one-on-one time. She and I went up to my room to talk. I told her everything about Logan, Alex, and Nikki, and how I wanted so much to end it with Logan to be with Ky.

"Jay, Sweetie, you need to do what you feel is right in your heart. I am surprised that you had chosen Ky; I never thought that would have occurred. I do, however, give my full support. I am pleased he treats you with respect and love. I can honestly say I have not seen him with anyone like he is with you. The way you two look at one another is how your father and I look at each other. I can see it was love at first sight for the both of you."

"I feel like whenever I am around Ky, I feel complete. I know he is where I belong. He doesn't do the things like Logan has done. He makes me feel special, makes me feel wanted, and makes me feel loved. The way he looks at me I just want to melt. I get weak in the knees. His smile, the way he winks at me, I have never had anyone make me feel the way that he does."

My phone rang. I went ahead and picked it up not paying any attention to the caller ID. It was Logan. I should have known. I knew I had already missed twenty-some calls of his.

"Jay, where the hell have you been?" He demanded.

"Logan, I have had important family matters going on, and I could not answer."

"It doesn't matter! I'm your family too! Have you forgotten that? You answer when I call you! You got that!"

I knew mom could hear everything he was saying her facial expressions went from shock to anger to disgust as he continued on. I was trying to explain to him when she grabbed the phone from me.

"Yes, Logan?" She said.

"Who the hell is this? Put Jay back on now!" He angrily demanded.

"No, the important issue she was trying to tell you was me, her Mother. And no man ever talks to my daughter the way you just had! If you think for one minute my daughter will marry someone like you, you have another thing coming! I will not allow it, and I am sure Sam will not allow it either. Oh, and another thing she was going to tell you, it is over; she has found someone who truly loves her and respects her. Move on, she is no longer with you." She hung up.

I was in awe of what she had done for me. I thanked her as a tear rolled down my cheek. I was finally free.

The phone rang continuously. I just let it go. I now had freedom again. I was far away, and he knew I found someone who does love me. I love Ky, and I will not let Logan try to get in the way of my happiness.

"Jay?" Ky said as he knocked on my door.

"Yes, Ky?" I said with a huge smile on my face as he walked in.

"We will be leaving tomorrow; I would like to spend some time with you before we head out. Shall we go for a walk?"

I immediately got up off the bed and walked over to him. He gave me a kiss and grabbed my hand. We headed off into the woods.

Chapter 8

"Milledge, prepare Darmel's former chamber; we may be having a guest soon." Helena requested.

"Yes, Your Majesty." He bowed, leaving the throne room.

Milledge was anxious to meet this girl, hoping he could somehow get her on his side as she was an outsider. Then he realized she would be the true High Queen. He was deciding what to do with her. Befriend her and use her to his advantage or off her. He learned from Enid she was born with the mark. What is it about this girl? What powers does she have? If only Millicent was able to see visions, she only had powers that were great but hardly used. He did not like her apprentice, Bray. He was too humble like the rest of Atlantis.

He went back to his chamber after preparing Darmel's' former chamber. He went to his sanctuary beneath his chambers. He needed to run some experiments and take care of Enid.

"Enid. Wake up. Have something to eat."

"Milledge, please, let me see my family again. I will not disclose anything from these last few years, what you have done and what you want to do. I want to tell them I love them and embrace them once more."

"We have discussed this before. You know I cannot take that

risk." He said as he had left her with a full meal and water.

"Milledge, please! I miss my family, my freedom! I cannot take this much more! Once, I had loved you. Now I hate you, and you have become someone who only thinks of himself! You are greedy. You never knew what love really was, even when it was in front of you before you decided to lock me away! I know you do not plan to keep me around. I have had this feeling all morning long. I know it's my time. If you will not let me see my family, then release me from this horrible life you have provided me with!"

Milldege stepped back into the room. He tried to make a move on her, but she refused him. He forcibly kissed her. She hated it. He then forced himself upon her, ravaging her. She cried, wishing he would stop. After a while, it ended.

"I hate you Milledge. I hate you for everything. You are not a true Atlantean! I wish you nothing but misery. And I will never disclose everything I know. I would rather take it with me to my death. I accept it. I know it's coming."

"If that is what you choose." Milledge then stood her up. Her ragged dress fell back down to her knees as he stood her up.

"I am a true Atlantean. Just because I had just taken you does not mean I am not. I wanted you once more, and I wanted you to feel me once more. I have plans for Atlantis, and the humans will be our servants."

She spat in his face.

"Very well then." He forcibly kissed her once more. She hated it; she hated him now after all he had done to her. She never knew what it was like to have hatred running through her until he had changed.

"I despise you for everything you have done. I wish you a life filled with nothing but misery, and I hope one day you are tortured like you have tortured me!"

Milledge knew he needed to test the creature's abilities. He decided now was the time he needed to get rid of Enid. He was tired of her not telling him everything and knew she was keeping things from him. Deep down, he still cared for her, but he cannot keep her like this anymore. He reminisced on the times they had once had, happiness and bliss. He knew she was weak. He grabbed her by the arm with force. Tears and fear filled her face, and she knew this was it.

He and Dylian created five Nibus altogether. Splicing Milledge's DNA, cobra, armadillo, bat, and a few other DNA from various amphibians and other species.

He led her by her arm, hurrying across the room; he opened the door and went to the left into the laboratory. At the far end of the laboratory was a large window and, to the right, a metal doorway. He opened the doorway, pushed her onto the landing on top of the stairway, and closed and locked the door. She was in fear; she stood up and looked down. She saw five-domed chambers; she could not make out what was in them with the thick, liquefied fluid in them. She turned around, banging on the doorway, begging Milledge to let her out, crying, not knowing what he was going to release. Terror overcame her.

Milledge walked over to the window. He waved his hand, and a screen appeared. He pressed a few things on it, then waved his hand away. He looked over at Enid. Tears started to fill his eyes, but he was holding back. She heard an opening of a chamber. She stood still, facing the doorway. She glanced to her right at the window where Milledge was; tears streaming down her face as he read her lips saying she still loved him. A few seconds later, she heard a hissing from behind her. Fear and terror were set in even more. She slowly turned around; standing in front of her was the most horrifying creature. She stared into its white eyes. It stood like a man, muscular like a man, full body black as night, hands that had sharp claws, talons for feet, skin hard as though you could not penetrate it, wings like a bat, no nose, no ears, it sensed with its forked tongue.

It hissed again, its tongue slithering in and out.

It then growled. It opened its mouth, showing its sharp, pointed teeth at the same time its cobra hood opened. It spewed sticky plasma-like saliva on her face, paralyzing her.

Enid's heartbeat raced. She knew her time was up. This was not how she wanted to go. She would have rather proceeded with her death by Milledge's own hands.

The creature raised its right arm; its claw quickly slashed her chest. It then sunk its teeth into her throat, ripping out a chunk of her neck. It spat it over the stairs and then started to drain her blood.

Milledge watched as he could no longer hold back the tears. He hated himself for what he had done. He still cared for her. He had let out only one and saw what damage they could do. He knew what he and Dylian had created was exactly what they were trying to accomplish.

Chapter 9

We had gotten back to the cabin after a nice long walk in the woods. It was refreshing, and I loved how Ky showed his affection by holding my hand, stopping every now and then, pulling me close to him, kissing me, and stoking my face with his hand. This felt so wonderful. Discussing the way of the Alantean life, how everyone is peaceful, there is no crime, and how everyone helps each other in need. They barter; they do not have coins or dollar bills. He described Atlantis to me how huge it seemed from how he was describing it. He was telling me how they do have weapons and certain ones do know defense moves. He had shown me a few, and while practicing, he grabbed me from behind, holding me, and then he kissed my neck. I wanted to melt.

I had my phone charging on the kitchen counter. As we were walking into the kitchen to get some water, the phone had rung.

"Hey Jay!"

"Nikki! Hey how are you?"

"Jay, what is going on? Logan is upset, crying his eyes out. I have never seen this man cry before; I mean, you know how he is all Mr. Macho and all. Alex had never seen him like this either. What's the deal? He won't talk about it other than saying how he can't live without you, blah, blah, blah. I know how you feel, but he does truly love you. I need the scoop."

"Nikki, I do not know where to begin. Um, well, for starters, my mother arrived out of nowhere."

"Shut up! Seriously? OMG! Wow! That's awesome! How are you getting along?"

"It's fantastic! I had always dreamed of this day, but I never knew that it would actually happen. The night she arrived; Logan called; I did not bother answering; meeting my mother for the first time was more important to me."

"Of course! No doubt about that."

"So earlier today, Logan called again, when I did finally answer, it was the same old Logan screaming at me for not answering and making me feel worthless as usual. Mom could hear him; she literally grabbed the phone from me, got on the phone and basically told him off."

"Jay, he is very sorry, and he wants to work this out. But I totally understand your side of everything, and I do not blame you, not after everything he had put you through, and you deserve better than that, Jay, you really do. You are very caring and sweet, beautiful; you have a lot to give. You deserve someone who will treat you with respect and love you for who you are. You have a lot going for you, Jay, don't forget that."

"Nikki, Logan is not what I want. I have met someone, and he makes me feel so special. And well I had fallen in love, and love at first sight. Like you had said before, it is a feeling like no other; it cannot be explained, feels like energy just running through your body, and when you know, you just know."

"Awe Jay! I am so happy for you! You deserve that, and you know I support you on this! You are my best friend, and I want you to be happy. Definitely forget Logan. He doesn't deserve you. Finding someone who makes you feel like you are special, their one and only, and you have that indescribable feeling is very rare, and when you find it, hold on to it, never let that go."

"Thank you, Nikki. I am sending Logan his ring back. I don't want it, and I don't want the reminder. I found the person who makes me feel complete and happy. It is everything about him, and I love how he looks at me, the winks, the smile, the way he touches me, kisses me, how he treats me, and makes me feel complete. When we look deep in each other's eyes, it's like he can see directly into my soul. I will not let him go. He had come to visit with Mom; he had never been here before, to, uh, North Carolina. He and his family are good friends with Mom, and she wanted to introduce us. And I am very grateful she had."

"Wow! That is awesome Jay! So, uh, don't you think it's a lil too soon? Then again, who am I to talk to? I felt that way with

Alex when I first saw him, so disregard that question."

I laughed. "I will. I do have to go. They are not here for long and will have to go back soon. I will talk to you soon, okay?"

"Okay Jay. I am very happy for you. Hugs, chica, will talk to you soon!"

"Bye!" I didn't have the heart to tell her I was possibly leaving for a while.

Dad, Mom and Ky were sitting in the living room in deep discussion. I went over and sat by Ky. He immediately grabbed my hand, holding it with both hands. I made my decision. As much as I would hate to leave Dad, I needed to go back with Mom and Ky. I gave them my decision. Dad looked so hurt, and I knew he wanted to cry. He came over and hugged me, knowing that tomorrow I would be leaving with them. We sat around laughing, telling times of our childhood and talked about many other things. I decided to go upstairs and start packing some things. As soon as I got to the stairs, I felt as though I couldn't breathe, and I felt as though I was burning up again. As soon as it came, it went. I don't know what this is, but I don't like it.

I walked over to the closet to grab some shirts. I looked into the mirror at the door. My whole body was engulfed in a fiery blue. I screamed so loud everyone bolted upstairs and into my room. I did not know what to do. Dad came over to grab my hand, and somehow, I had burnt him; he screamed in pain.

"Daddy! I'm so sorry!" I cried. I didn't know how to control this. I kept asking why this was happening to me. I wanted this to disappear, everything, the visions, the teleportation (although kinda cool) or whatever you wanted to call it. I was done with it. They were all staring at me in surprise. I kept wishing for it to go away and see how badly Dad had been hurt. He was grabbing his right hand, grunting in pain and looking at me, knowing he could not help me. No sooner was I wishing it away, it was gone. I went over to Dad immediately.

I grabbed Dad's arm, his hand was severely burned; his skin was bubbly, and it was the most disturbing thing I have ever seen. I had the urge to put my hand over it, but Dad stopped me.

"Don't touch it sweetie. We need to go to the hospital; this is bad; the pain is too much."

"Dad, please, I have an urge to place my hand over it; I cannot resist it."

He looked at me dumbfounded. They all did.

"Sam let her. I do not know why, but allow it." Mother had told him.

Dad looked at me and nodded his head in approval. I placed my hand over the burned area. I kept telling myself I wanted to heal him. I started to feel a coolness come all over me. My hand I had placed on Dad's arm began to glow a yellowish white. Dad's suffering was easing up. The energy I was feeling was intense. As soon as I felt drained, I let go. I started to fall backwards; Ky ran over and caught me before I fell onto the floor. He picked me up and carried me over to the bed.

"Oh my! It's healed! Jay, you healed it!" Dad said in amazement. "Sweetie, are you alright?"

"Yeah, I just feel drained. I need to rest. I think." I rolled over onto my right side, facing the window. I started to look out the window at the tree branch and closed my eyes.

"She is not leaving unless I go, Luciana. I cannot let my baby, who is going through all this, just up and leave. She needs me and I can't let her go, not knowing if she keeps going through these things."

"Sam, it would not be allowed. Let us go somewhere and discuss this."

"Ky. You are the Prince. Can you not allow this?"

"Unfortunately, I cannot, Sam. The decision is not up to me. It is my Mother's decision. Only Jaycenda can come."

"Let Jaycenda rest. And yes, Luciana, let's go downstairs and discuss this. I do not want to talk about it here in her room. She needs her rest."

"I will stay with her and make sure she is safe," Ky stated, looking over at me with a concerned look on his face.

"Normally, I would not allow it. But due to the events that have been take place, I will permit it."

Dad and mom left the room. Although I had my eyes closed, I could hear them. I felt Ky climb into bed with me and wrap his arms around me, pulling me close to him. I wanted to open my eyes, and I wanted to say something, but I was so drained I could not do either. I felt safe in his arms and drifted off to sleep.

Hours later, I awoke to still being held tightly by Ky and his hand holding mine. I got the biggest smile. I have never felt such comfort or felt so safe. I let go of his hand and rolled over, facing him and put my arm around him. He had opened his eyes and looked into mine, smiling. He kissed my forehead.

"Did you sleep well? You gave us all a scare."

"Yes, I had. I feel great, actually, waking up next to you. I am happy."

"Good, I am happy as well." He smiled as we looked into each other's eyes. This time, I made the first move and kissed him. Things were getting more intense, and then a knock on the door. Lovely, I hated being interrupted in this moment.

The door opened, and dad walked on in. He cleared his throat. By the look on his face, he did not like seeing Ky and I holding each other. Thankfully, we still had clothes on.

"Jay, how are you feeling?"

"I feel great!" I said smiling.

"Uh huh. Well, would you both please come downstairs?"

"Yes Dad."

Dad looked at Ky like he had done something wrong. I did not like that. However, the look was not as bad as some of the ones he had given Logan.

Ky held my hand as we went downstairs. Mom and Dad sat in the recliners facing the couch. Ky and I snuggled up on the couch, his arm around me. Dad turned the television off. The sun was setting, and the lights were dimmed.

"Jaycenda, your father and I have had a long conversation while you were sleeping. I wish I could allow him to come with us. The High Queen will not permit it until the time has come for Atlantis to rise. We leave tomorrow. Your father does not want you to come with your recent discoveries of yourself. We felt it was ultimately your decision to come with Ky and I or remain here with Sam until it is time. I wish for you to come with us. It has been wonderful to see you and getting to know you. Your powers are growing and can be dangerous. I have only had these last two days and only a few weeks with you when you were born. I would love nothing more than you to choose to come with us."

I did not know what to say. I looked over at Dad, and he looked like he wanted to cry. I honestly do not know what to do at this point now with everything going on. Dad has always been there for me, and he has always been my rock. This was the first time I have had the chance to see my mother, hug her, speak to her, and get to know her, and now I have the chance to leave with her. I was torn. I did not want to make the choice. I could not take Dad with me, and mom and Ky could not stay; they needed to return. Well, this just sucks! Ky held me. I started shaking.

"I hate this, just to let you know. I don't want to leave dad behind, and I know you both must return tomorrow. I do not know what to do. Dad, you have always been there for me, and Mom, this is the first time we actually met and talked and all. I just…this is all so sudden. But…"

I looked over at Ky, and he nodded at me, letting me know that whatever decision I made, he would support me on it.

"But I think I am going to stay here with Dad. Its July, December is not too far off. I do not want to disappoint you, Mom or you, Ky. If Dad cannot come, I choose to stay. I will miss you both dearly. I cannot believe I am choosing this because I finally have been able to get to know you Mother, and I finally found happiness and love." I said, looking over at Ky with tears in my eyes and smiling.

"I will wait for you," Ky said to me and kissed me.

"And I promise to wait for you as well," I told him as I hugged him and kissed him back.

"I am disappointed, but I respect your decision." Luciana had said. She came over crying and hugging me.

We spent the night talking over the next few hours. Dad realized how happy Ky and I were. He had told us Ky and I could spend the last night together. It felt weird Dad had said that.

Ky and I pulled out the sleeper sofa in the room where we first made love, and I did not want to be anywhere near my parents. This was pretty far away enough from them. I was dreading the morning, but for the time being, I was enjoying my time with Ky and the most wonderful night spent in his arms.

Chapter 10

Within the next few days I was yearning to see Mom and Ky again. Wondering they had made it back safely.

Dad and I were having dinner when the doorbell rang. Dad said he wasn't expecting anyone. I then remembered after Mom and Ky left Nikki had asked for my address and was going to try to make it down.

I answered the door. To my surprise, it was Nikki and Alex. I immediately stepped through the doorway, giving them each a hug. Then I heard someone clearing their throat. I looked to my left, and there was Logan standing there a few feet away. I did not go running to him; I remained neutral.

"I'm sorry, Jay, he was the only way we were able to get down here to see you," Nikki said.

"A warning would have been nice," I said angrily.

"I know, and again, I apologize; Alex and I just wanted to surprise you though."

"I know, and I am thankful he brought you here," I said, giving Logan a look of disgust.

"Jay, I am so sorry for everything I have done to you. I am trying my best to change. Please believe that! It killed me when you told Nikki and your mom stating you were with someone else. I want you back. I know there is distance, but I will move here; I'll find a place in town. Please, Jay, give me another chance."

"You had numerous chances, Logan. The damage has been done. You cannot repair what has happened. Yes, I have found someone else. I can honestly say I now know what love feels like. I don't love you; I didn't know what it was like until now. You will not get me back this time, Logan." I turned around and walked inside. They all walked in with their bags.

Dad walked into the living room, surprised to see Logan. You could tell by the look on his face that anger was building up in him. He was giving Logan the look of death, fists getting tighter and tighter and his face getting redder by the second.

"Hello, Nikki and Alex; you two are welcome here. Logan, you are not. You hurt my little girl once too many times. She found someone else."

"I understand that. I do love her, and I am changing. Please allow me to stay, or I am going to have to take Nikki and Alex back with me now."

Dad was angry but knew how much I had wanted to see Nikki and Alex since we moved here.

"Fine, but you are staying on the couch. The spare bedroom will be for Nikki and Alex. There will be no back talk, no disrespecting Jaycenda or me, or anyone who is in this house. She is done with you. Don't try to win her back."

"I understand, Mr. Spencer." He replied with his eyes welled up. I had never seen Logan seem so sincere, let alone about to cry.

The week passed. It was great to see Nikki and Alex. I had the given the ring back to Logan. Surprisingly, Logan had been decent and respective. He did try to kiss me goodbye; I, however, was not having it and pushed him away. I told them to come down before December 10th for the week. I did not discuss the reasoning behind it simply explained I wanted to spend time with them close to the holiday. They said they would be here. Although going to miss my birthday on October 2nd, at least I know they will be safe when everything happens. It was nice to see Logan as a new person. However, he had already done the damage. There is no turning back. I love Ky and the wait for him is worth it. I can't seem to get him off my mind. At least I know our paths will cross again soon, along with my mother.

Chapter 11

The months have flown by. It was strange to have a blizzard at the end of August. That was only the beginning. Soon after the blizzard, more of Mother Nature's disasters began to occur more often. Hurricanes one after another, tornados touching down across the states and other countries, at times multiple tornados at once. Massive tsunamis hit the West Coast. Many fled and many did not survive. It is now December 5th. The destruction will only get worse. I pray Nikki and Alex are able to make it here safely before the big destruction happens.

Nikki called. They were on their way; they had gotten held up a day caught in a bad snowstorm and were a few hours away. I hoped they were going to make it; that same storm is heading our way and the mountains are not the greatest to be driving on. I prayed they would make it here soon.

Dad had spent the last several months stocking up on food, water and clothing. I guess you might want to say he is a prepper. Anything you could think of that he thought we would need, he had it.

They finally arrived right before the storm was due to hit our area. We sat down in front of the fireplace, catching up on the last few months and having a lot of laughs. Over the last few months, I continued to have the visions, and I had finally controlled being in one place and then appearing in another. It was pretty cool. I was actually enjoying having that power, although I could not go very far from my surroundings. I have not had another episode where I felt like I was on fire and had the bluish fire surrounding me.

Dad and I finally broke down and told them why we wanted them here at this time and the importance of it.

"Bullshit Jay!" Logan yelled. "That whole Mayan calendar thing we have been hearing about is a joke! You don't have any special powers! There will not be any mass destruction! And Atlantis is not real! It is merely a myth! Have you and your father gone insane?" He said in such anger.

I looked at him in anger.

"Oh really Logan? So this is a joke?" I concentrated on willing myself to the kitchen. Poof, there I was.

"Holy Shit!" Logan, Nikki, and Alex yelled all at the same time and in awe. The look on their faces was priceless.

"How? Wha.?" Nikki did not have any words to say. All three still had their mouths dropped.

"It is not a joke Logan. This is for real. Dad has a secret room that is stocked up. We went over this. There is going to be massive destruction, and Atlantis will rise. The Mayan calendar was not exactly saying it was the end of the world, somewhat yes. There will be a lot of changes. The actual date had already been destroyed in the Mayan Codices. Your families, I am sorry to say will not make it. I haven't seen any visions of them, just of all the destruction."

"So you mean to tell me you only invited us but not our families?" Nikki questioned in anger.

"I only had enough to get supplies for all of us and only enough room for us. I am sorry." Sam said to all of them.

They all had the look of anger mixed with sorrow. They pulled out their phones and started calling their loved ones to tell them how much they loved them, but with the storm hitting hard now, there was no service. They each took a turn calling from the landline.

It was now December 11th. We were all getting our things together in the shelter. Logan was trying to get me to be with him again, making statements like "this could be our last time on earth" blah, blah, blah. It so was not happening. I kept thinking of Ky. He and I had taken a picture together before he left, and I also had one of Mom and I and one with a group picture of all of us. Love the camera had a timer on it. I had always kept those pictures close to me, especially of Ky. Logan saw the picture. He did not like seeing it, but he needed to deal with it and move on.

Dad called Trish earlier in the morning. She also thought the end was near. She had packed her things and her rations. She braved the storm as bad as the roads were to be with us. The normal ten-minute drive for her was more like a forty-five-minute drive. Nikki, Alex, and Logan continued to take turns on the landline, calling everyone they could get ahold of.

It was now getting late into the evening. I was getting this tingling sensation all over.

"Uh, everyone, I know it is not tomorrow yet, but I think we need to get to the shelter, and we need to go now," I told them.

"Well, whatever Jay says, I say we do," Alex spoke up. "Jay, I know we were angry with you and Sam about our families not being here with us. But I think I speak for all of us when I say thank you for having us here."

"Yes, thank you," Nikki said in a low tone. I knew she was still upset.

"What exactly are you all talking about?" Trish asked.

"You will see Trish." Dad insisted.

Logan then spoke up. "I agree, but I wish you would give me another chance, Jay. I miss us."

"Not gonna happen Logan. Now let's get going. This feeling is getting stronger."

We headed down to the shelter. On the way, we started to feel tremors. We hurried to the doorway and closed it. It was only the beginning of what was to come.

Chapter 12

Cities came tumbling down. Rivers and oceans started to flood cities. Earthquakes worldwide, tornados touching down all over Europe, the United States, Australia, and China. Desert storms in Egypt and other countries. The super Volcanoes Erupted, the largest in Yellowstone, was massive taking out a majority of the Western United States. Exploding with massive ash and lava destroying everything in its path. Hawaii and other islands are gone, with volcanoes erupting and tsunamis overtaking. It was the day of destruction.

During the disasters Atlantis was slowly rising from the Abyss. A very large whirlpool occurred where Atlantis was rising. Once it had risen, the dome remained intact.

After two days of the destruction worldwide, heavy ash continued to cover the atmosphere. The sky remained in total blackness.

All ships left Atlantis to save those who survived. Many were struggling to survive as oxygen was scarce. The ships were equipped to locate any survivors, including those who were underground or hiding in caves.

Daj accompanied Luciana and Ky to retrieve Jaycenda and Sam. Luciana received a vision that they were safe and had others with them. She knew they would be. She also knew she had to have Jaycenda go to Egypt to the Great Pyramid before returning to Atlantis. She was not sure as to why, but she had seen a vision that she needed to take her; it was vague, but she knew Jaycenda had great powers.

Luciana, Ky and Daj recovered several survivors before going to get Jaycenda, Sam, and the others.

The ship flew over the rubble of the cabin and right above where the shelter was. A beam had shot down. Luciana and Ky stood on the circular pad toward the back of the ship. The survivors watched in awe as Daj pulled a screen up touched a few buttons, and they were gone.

Everyone was asleep, crammed in one room in sleeping bags, air mattresses and the sleeper sofa.

Luciana and Ky appeared.

"We are here," Ky announced loudly, waking everyone and walking over toward me.

I was on the air mattress. I woke to his voice I was so happy I got the biggest smile on my face. As I was trying to sit up, he leaned in, hugging and kissing me. Logan looked at us in disgust. I didn't care; I had my love in front of me. Mom was hugging and kissing Dad and walked over to hug me and kissed my cheek.

Nikki and Alex were slowly waking up. Trish was looking at them in complete amazement, wondering what exactly was going on.

We gathered our bags. I hurried up and freshened up a bit, as well as Nikki and Trish. Hey, we are women. We gotta keep our appearance up.

We boarded the ship, and off we went. We picked up other survivors until the ship was full. It held up to around one hundred people. Mom stated all ships were sent out to gather the survivors. She stated that Atlantis was massive and had room for thousands of survivors. She said many will have to learn to live together as there are many housing complexes it is nothing like the world we once knew. She was not sure exactly how many survivors there would be.

She stated she made sure our quarters were located inside the palace as I was now the designated Queen. I was not quite sure how I felt about that. I felt uneasy. Here I am with this birthmark that gave me powers and automatically made me a queen.

Mom also filled me in before we were to head to Atlantis that we needed to go to Egypt. The peak of the Great Pyramid was peeking out of the sand.

Daj hovered over the peak. I glanced out the window as a loud noise occurred. Daj had the screen up, pushing a few buttons. All of a sudden, sand started to swirl around and move outward from the pyramid until it was completely revealed. He moved the ship over to the entrance to the pyramid.

Mom explained to me that I needed to make my way to the Queen's Chamber. She was not as to why it was a vision she had seen. She had pulled up a 3D dimension of the layout of the pyramid. I went to the portal, and it shot me down into the pyramid. It was dark, and the space was tight. I concentrated on the time I had the blue fiery glow. I wanted to have that now so I could see.

I became hot all over. I looked down at my hands; I was having the blue fire again. I finally made my way to the Queen's chamber. There were areas where I had to crawl. My instinct was to stand in the middle of the chamber. I went to the middle of the chamber. I felt hotter than I already was, and I felt paralyzed. I was hurting all over; light beams from each shaft on my right and left shot directly into me. The pain worsened, but I could not move except to arch my back and scream. A huge light beam came from me as I looked toward the ceiling and shot straight up into the ceiling.

Luciana, Ky, Daj and some of the survivors watched in amazement as two beams were shooting into the pyramid and one shooting straight out of the peak of the pyramid. The thick ash covering the atmosphere was swirling around and shooting straight up into the beam that was coming from the peak and into space.

After a long while, the sky became clear as it had once been and a pleasant blue.

"Daj, get me down there now!" Luciana demanded as she grabbed a long crystal stick from a compartment. When she grabbed it, it had lit up. The survivors were mumbling amongst themselves.

Daj motioned for her to head to the portal.

Luciana appeared in the pyramid and found her way to the Queen's chamber. She saw Jaycenda lying on the floor, looking lifeless. She ran over to her, dropping the crystal stick beside Jaycenda. Her heart was breaking, and she was crying. She rolled Jaycenda over as she was kneeling beside her. She lifted her halfway up, cradling her head and upper body. Jaycenda was still breathing, but barely.

"Oh, my child! Please stay with me!" She cried out. "I lost you for many years. I cannot bear to lose you permanently! Please, sweetheart, wake up!" She begged.

Jaycenda slowly opened her eyes. "Mom." She said weakly. "I want to get out of here."

"I know, but you are too weak right now to make it back to the entrance."

"I want to be on the ship and away from here," Jaycenda repeated herself as she closed her eyes. Jaycenda was willing herself and her mother to be on the ship.

She used the last of her strength to get them on the ship.

Luciana immediately called for Ky to come to help her get Jaycenda into the healing chamber.

Logan demanded he help, but Ky and Luciana was not having it. Sam was holding Logan back as much as he wanted to be the one helping to move her.

Logan became frantic and blamed them for the condition Jaycenda was in.

Ky hurriedly carried Jaycenda to the chamber and laid her down in it. He kissed her and told her to come back to him. He closed the clear hatch over the cylinder shaped chamber. He placed his hands on the chamber. Sam and her friends came over.

"My baby, come back to us," Sam said, crying as he placed his hands on the chamber. Everyone close to her was crying and wishing her well.

Chapter 13

They returned to Atlantis. Since Jaycenda had miraculously cleared the sky from all the ash that covered the world, the air was pure and crisp again. The dome, however, still surrounded Atlantis.

The ship landed in the landing port. Luciana went over to check on Jaycenda. Below the hatch door, a light had gone from red to green. She was relieved. She opened the hatch. Jaycenda had awakened.

"Mom," I said as I tried to sit up.

Luciana helped her sit up.

"Take it easy, sweetie, you have been through a lot. We are here in Atlantis now. We are still on the ship, and the survivors are now getting off first."

"I need to talk to you, Mom. So much happened in there, and I do not know what to make of it."

"In time. We need to go to the Coliseum before going to the palace."

"There is a Coliseum here?"

"Yes. There are many things here. You will soon see."

Ky came over, gave me a hug and kissed me softly. "My love, you had me worried. I do not know what my life would be like without you. It was already hard enough when we left not to have you by my side the last few months."

"Jay, please come back to me. This guy is a fool. He doesn't know you like I do. You met for a brief time; this isn't right! He can't love you like I do!" Logan cried out, walking over toward me.

I continued to stay in Ky's arms. Ky was giving Logan a stern look and told him to stay away from me.

"Logan, he loves me more than you ever have. Accept the fact that we are through. You could never love me or respect me like Ky does. He is genuine, and he is sweet. He does not treat me the way that you had. I love him, and that is the end of it. Deal with it."

Logan lowered his head, and Dad came over to hug me intensely. Logan looked up at me with tears in his eyes. "I really do love you, Jay." And walked away.

Daj had the remaining survivors off the ship and was then getting us prepared to get off the ship and onto the landing field. Thousands of people were getting off ships in the landing field, talking amongst themselves and discussing how amazing this all was. I heard one person say this is a new beginning. That it is.

Mom, Dad, Ky, Alex, Nikki, Logan, Trish, Daj, and I started to walk toward a building that had few windows and looked made of stone. The dome still covering Atlantis was amazing, the pink, purple, bluish color and producing its own sunlight. It was stunning, nonetheless. I looked to the left and up toward the palace. I saw the pyramid-shaped peak on top of the palace where the plasma light was creating the dome, shooting straight up, almost like how it was when I was in the Great Pyramid. The palace was sitting on top of the mountain. You could tell it was huge and could tell the architecture was a cross between ancient Greek and Egyptian. This was truly amazing. I noticed there were pillars with archways leading from the palace entrance to the cliff to the long stairwell down to an arched bridge. It was at a distance from where we were at. On the way toward the building, we made a left; there was a platform of some type. The survivors were walking past the building as Daj told us to get on the platform. We got on the platform; it was hovering over the water.

We made our way over toward the bridge and landed on the edge of the bank near the Coliseum. The survivors were making their way through a huge garden and straight over to the Coliseum. Ky said the garden was called the Artilla. He promised to take me there later. The Coliseum looked very much like the one you saw pictures of in Rome. However, this one was intact. It had colors of red designs throughout, and the pillars were green. You could hear someone singing from inside sounding like opera, but it was very angelic and soothing.

Ky had us enter through a back way and into an open boxed

area where the royals sat. The Coliseum was filling up with many survivors. In the middle of the Coliseum a child was the one who was singing. I would say she was probably around fifteen with blonde hair. I asked Ky who she was he said her name was Vix. He did not know much about her, only that she had the most amazing voice in Atlantis.

When she had finished, she left the arena. A screen appeared with a woman's face; she was beautiful, and her hair was pinned up wearing a crown. Ky stated that it was his mother.

"Greetings, survivors and welcome to Atlantis. I am Helena, the High Queen. We welcome you with open arms. Words cannot describe the loss of loved ones and the destruction that had occurred. The world is in healing. We Atlanteans live in peace and Harmony. We do not tolerate crime or any violence of any sort. We work together. You were brought here to keep your race surviving and to make the world a better place. We will teach you everything to rebuild your lives and to do so without hatred toward anyone. We have plenty of room for all. You will learn to live together; some families will be sharing housing. Everyone is expected to work together. Take time leaving the Coliseum. We have workers who will be assisting you on where you will be staying and explain our way of life. Be patient; there are many of you. There are many workers outside the Coliseum waiting, so please depart slowly." And she disappeared.

"Well, now it's time to head to the palace." Ky insisted.

We left the Coliseum the same way we came in and got back on the platform. I was amazed at how it held all of us. It still hovered and went straight over to the edge of the mountain and straight up to the cliff. The palace was bigger than what it looked from a distance. We made our way to the entrance and a servant named Milledge greeted us and took us each to our living quarters. He explained that our belongings were already placed so we did not need to wonder where they may have been.

All of our living quarters were on the same level and not far from each other. Ky, however, had Logan's placed near Milledge's. He wanted nothing more than to not have Logan anywhere near Jaycenda, but the housing complexes were already expected to be filled with the other survivors.

Milledge first showed Logan to his quarters, then Nikki and Alex, Trish, Dad, and finally me. Dad wanted some alone time with Mom. I could see some jealousy with Trish. And I wanted some alone time with Ky; however, Ky said he needed to go speak with his mother and that I would be meeting with her and my mother soon.

I walked into the living quarters. All the doors were metallic. The sitting area was adorned in gold trim fluffy, looking seats, and no television well, that just sucks. Oh well, more time spent with

Ky. I made my way down a small hallway to my right; there was a doorway, but this one was wooden, not metallic. Yay! I found the bathroom. I continued straight down to another doorway. Milledge was behind me the whole time, talking to me and explaining that all meals everyone eats together in the dining hall. I opened the doorway, and it was a huge bedroom large feather mattress with gold trim around the room. It was decorated with the most unusual murals and drapery, just beautiful. Only disappointment was there were no windows.

Milledge and I talked about many things. He seemed pretty cool. His long, curly hair suited him. I asked him why he was a servant he said his family always has for a very long time. He said each Atlantean has a specific job they do. There is no currency; it is mainly barter. He discussed the market area and the pub his Aunt Millicent owned. He said I should try some of the ale and wine and to play a game called Dilent. I asked what exactly was, and he said it was a board on the wall; a small dot will move around, and you gotta try to hit it with pretty much a dart from what he was explaining. The more you hit it the faster it got, and the more points added up. Pretty much all-in fun for free drinks. Milledge and I talked a bit more, and he had to leave. I looked forward to speaking with him again.

Ky walked in as Milledge was leaving. Perfect timing! Now I get some alone time with my man!

"Milledge, Mother would like to see you."

"Thank you, Ky. I will attend to her now."

Chapter 14

Milledge knocked on the doorway of the High Queen's chamber.

Helena opened the door. "Do come in and have a seat, please." She said hesitantly.

"You're Majesty, what is wrong?" He asked as he watched her pacing back and forth, fidgeting with her fingers.

"Milledge, I need to talk to someone. I cannot discuss this with Kyrie as he is in love with that girl!"

"Your Majesty, this girl you are referring to is Luciana's daughter, your dearest friend. Why act like this toward the girl? You have yet to meet her. She seems very charming." Milledge started wondering what Helena was about to say. This could put his plan more into motion.

"Milledge, you do not understand! She is now here! Only few Atlanteans know of the "mark". We kept a lot of things secret for a very long time. Anyone born with the mark of two intertwined half-moons is the true heir to the throne. I am no longer the chosen one. Once she arrived in Atlantis, the charmed necklace got hot and fell off I cannot get it back on. I tried to go into the labyrinth, but it won't glow. When I went to the crystal to gain knowledge with Luciana, it would not provide exactly what I wanted to know; it gave details of our past, with us originating from Mars and making Earth our home, helping the cultures here develop and passing some of our knowledge on. It showed that anyone who has the "mark" is the true heir with great powers. I know we need to get her to get rid of this dome. But I do not want to give up my place at the throne! I have ruled Atlantis for many years since my father's passing. I cannot imagine giving it up now unless I was on my deathbed and passing the reigns onto my son! This girl has no clue about our way of life! She has no clue how to rule a citadel! She would ruin everything that we have strived for! I just do not know what to do." She finally sat down, buried her head in her hands and began to cry.

Milledge began to ponder putting a plan into place. Only few knew of his plans. This would be perfect Helena does not want to give up the thrown and already dislikes this girl. He was thinking.

"Well, then. What do you suppose we do? You dislike the girl and obviously do not like the fact Kyrie is in love with her."

"Oh, that is another thing. She started calling him Ky, and he prefers that over his given name."

"This is interesting. You don't want to give up the throne, then don't."

"It is not that easy, Milledge. It's the necklace. Once it is near her, it will leave my hand and attach itself to her. When the necklace chooses you, you are the ruler. However, if maybe something happened to her, I can go back to being High Queen again."

"So are you suggesting we off her?"

"Milledge, I am. Do not breathe a word. I cannot allow my son to know of these plans. Come, let me show you that I do appreciate you and want your help." She seduced Milledge, and he loved every second of it. Never had he though Helena would have these thoughts, let alone be with her.

They lay in bed discussing possible ways to get rid of Jaycenda. Knowing it would be too suspicious if it were to occur right away. Time was needed.

"Well I guess it is time to talk to the girl and get this dome gone finally. Milledge, be a dear and get the girl."

"But of course." He said with a smirk as they were both getting dressed.

Milledge left to get Jaycenda. He was amazed at how Helena is taking all this, and he never thought she would feel this way about giving up the throne, let alone seduce him. He was having his day, and it felt pretty good.

He knocked on the door. It took a few minutes, but Ky finally answered the door shirtless.

"Sorry if coming in bad timing; your mother wishes to speak

with Jaycenda."

"Oh, um yeah, I'll go get her to come in and have a seat."

Milledge stepped in but did not sit down.

Ky came back into the bedroom.

"Who is that?"

"Milledge. Mother wishes to meet with you now. As much as I would rather we stay here and make love, it's best not to keep Mother waiting."

"Okay. I'll get dressed, and we will go to her. I am looking forward to meeting her."

"I'm sure she is looking forward to meeting you as well." He said as he grabbed my hand, kissed it and then pulled me into him, kissing me passionately. "I want to marry you, soon." He smiled and cupped my face, and I just melted. This feeling of being in love was the greatest feeling anyone could ever have.

Ky and I made our way to the High Queen's chamber. Ky did not knock; he opened the door and walked in holding my hand. He introduced us. She seemed pleasant, but something seemed off at the same time.

She was tightly clutching something in her hands. It was almost as though whatever she had; she did not want to let go.

We all sat down in the sitting room, Helena across from us. She was telling me of a necklace that, when her father passed the necklace had chosen her to be the High Queen, how it chooses the first born. If something should happen to the first born, if they had a child, it would choose them; if no child, then it would choose the second-born sibling in line to the throne.

Helena discussed about the one who has the "mark" that, for some reason, they are the true heir to the throne. I could tell she didn't like discussing this, the look on her face. She seemed uneasy talking about it. She unclutched her hands the necklace sprung out of her hands and wrapped itself around my neck.

"What the?" I said in astonishment. I had no idea what to make of this.

"As I thought, you are the true heir." Helena said in a sadden tone.

"But what if I do not want this? What if I wanted you to take this thing back?"

"No, my dear. It chose you. It does not matter if you do not wish to be the High Queen. This is your destiny."

"I'm so sorry Helena. Honestly, this is not what I want."

"Well first thing is first. You are the only one who can remove the dome. Do not ask as to how; I do not know."

There was a knock on the door. Ky opened the door Asher and Arileen advised they needed to speak with Helena immediately. They came in, explaining that they had the same vision. Jaycenda needed to go to the throne room and stand in the middle of the circle.

"Well then, let's see what kind of powers you have, dear." Helena said with a sinful smile.

We approached the Throne room. I felt drawn to the circle like I had been drawn to the center of the Great Pyramid. I stood in the middle of the odd design. Around the circle were etchings like the ones on the headband and the metal box the crystal had fit in when Dad had first shown them to me.

Looking at the etchings, I started to get into a trance. I could hear myself speaking in another tongue as I was reading these etchings around the circle. The circled floor and design started to illuminate. There was some shaking of the palace, but nothing to be too concerned about. It was very old and built to last. After a few minutes, the illumination ended.

"Um….well, that felt weird. What was I saying?"

"That is in ancient language we no longer use. I am not sure what you were saying." Helena advised.

We all left the palace and went outside into the courtyard. Mom and Dad were already outside telling how the plasma descended into the crystal peak on top of the palace. Looking up, you could see bright blue sky and the real sun. The dome was no longer. You could smell the sea and, in the distance, hear the waves crashing against the walls surrounding Atlantis.

Helena, Ky, and Milledge were taking this all in, and I am sure all the Atlanteans were. This was a very long time in the making for them to have been freed from it.

You could hear in the distance screams of joy, drums and horns. It was a great feeling to know you have done something that has made a lot of people happy.

Ky grabbed me and pulled me close to him, kissing my forehead. I looked over at his mother. She looked saddened yet angry. I do not know what to make of her; I did not care for her. That opinion I was keeping to myself. Her expressions changed whenever Ky, Mom or Dad looked over toward her. Talk about putting on a fake smile, and I should know I was the master behind them.

"Hey beautiful. I promised you I would take you to the Artilla Gardens later. Looks like it will be sunset soon, and I want to spend my first sunset in Atlantis with my love in Artilla."

I loved how he looked at me and those green almond-shaped eyes of his. We went around the palace and over to the platform. This thing was wicked fun. Once it dropped above water and hovered over to the bank on the tier, he lifted me up and carried me into the gardens. It was so beautiful. Unusual plant life and flowers I had never seen before, nor did they seem to be from our time or planet. Mini waterfalls were all over the place, and of blue colored stone benches. We chose one by the largest of the mini waterfalls, surrounded by some tropical plant life and some of the unusual plants and flora. Listening to the music playing in the distance, you could practically hear the people dancing in the streets. We looked up to the sky, watching it turn pink and orange, and then to night, watching the stars. The whole time holding one another, I felt at peace; it felt like I really was home.

Chapter 15

Milledge was walking back to his chamber when he saw Logan pacing back and forth.

"What is wrong?" He asked, looking at Logan with interest as to what is going on.

"I want Jaycenda back, and I am trying to figure out how to get her back. She is the one woman that I love, and she belongs with me!"

Milledge listened to Logan rant and rave. He didn't like him. When he had conversed with Jaycenda earlier in the day about Atlantis, he had asked her why Ky did not want him near any of them, and she had explained their past. How he had been abusive towards her emotionally and verbally. He could tell this guy was a joke. As of right now, he had to play his game right with Jaycenda and be her "friend". Hmmm. He was thinking to himself this Logan can possibly get in the way. Would anyone really notice him being missing? Milledge had his evil grin come across his face.

"You know Logan, why don't we go into my chamber and discuss this more?"

"Yeah. Sure. I guess. You seem to be about the only one who will actually talk to me. I could use a new friend.

Milledge told him to follow him as they headed into his

sleeping chamber; Logan said, "Whoa there, buddy! I do not swing that way!"

"I do not know what you are talking about I was simply going to show you my sanctuary." He said as he walked over to the bull's head and pushed it in, opening the wall.

"Duh…yeah that's cool! That's cool! Yeah, let's go check it out!"

Milledge was thinking to himself how this boy had no idea what he was in for.

They continued to his laboratory, and Logan was in amazement at everything. How this place was hidden, and no one knew about it. They proceeded over to a doorway. Milledge opened the doorway slightly.

"Go ahead. I will be behind you shortly."

"Coolio. This is pretty awesome. I get to check some things out."

Logan preceded through the doorway. Milledge quickly shut and locked the door.

"What? Why did you lock the door?"

Logan looked over to the window to see Milledge have an intriguing smile and waving to him. He was hearing growling not sure where it was coming from. He looked around and saw nothing, but several chambers like Jaycenda had been in, only standing up right. One of them opened and seeing four more, seeing the thick liquid being drained and seeing the creatures that were in them. The chambers all at once were slowly opening. Logan began pounding on the door, begging to be let out. Asking what he had done. He was in fear, and Milledge was enjoying this.

Logan felt himself being picked up from under his shoulders. Whatever it was that had grabbed him was flying. Fear set in even more. He saw four creatures stepping away from the chambers. Seeing their forked tongues slithering in and out, making these awful noises to one another. They all looked up toward him. The one that had grabbed him made the same noise back to them as if they were communicating. Suddenly, it let go of Logan. He fell hard to the floor on his stomach. Scared and sore, he quickly looked around to the wall towards the stairs and looked up to the window, seeing Milledge watching with delight. Under the window where Milledge was standing, there looked to be some type of stoned doorway with unusual etchings on it. He was not sure how it would open. He tried to crawl over toward it only to feel something grabbed his legs, flip him over onto his back and dragging him. He looked at his legs, seeing this creature dragging him toward the others. He heard all the growls and hissing. Another came over, bent down over top of him, looking at him, the tongue slithering in and out. Logan had never been so frightened in his life. He saw the cobra hood appear and the creature spitting plasma-like saliva on his face. He was paralyzed. He could not move. His heartbeat raced. He felt the claws of the creatures tearing into him and tearing him apart. His last thoughts were of how much he really did love Jaycenda and how sorry he was for everything.

Milledge was quite pleased with himself. He went back up to his quarter. He waved his hand in the air, and a screen appeared. He was contacting Dylian, wanting him to come over.

Dylian appeared within a timely manner. Milledge had discussed how he had to get rid of Enid and what he had just done with Logan.

"I am truly amazed. All of our work has paid off. These creatures, with your help, will get me where I need to be."

"Yes Milledge. I hope everything will go according to plan. However, I must warn you recently the twin seers met with Helena several months ago. I had just been informed of this. I think they somehow may have an idea. I know Millicent has casted her spells to protect us. However, they had mentioned to her they had a vision that she needed to have the splicing engineers to create some of the creatures from years past. Centaurs, harpies, mermaids, and Pegasus. They were told not to have me informed of these, as to why I do not know. I am the head engineer. I have no access to try to stop these creatures from developing, and I am not sure if they have already been developed. I overheard two others discussing this. That is how I know. How many I do not know. The laboratory that I believe they are in has my access is denied."

"Well, this is going to be a fun show now, isn't it?"

"Yes, I believe so. When do you plan to release all the Nibus?"

"In time. I should fill you in. Helena is not happy about Kyrie, rather Ky, as he now likes to be called. He is in love with Luciana's daughter. She has the "mark" of the intertwined half-moons. She is the rightful heir, which makes me cringe. Helena is not happy about her having to step down as High Queen and Jaycenda taking her place. She knows Ky loves her, but she wants her gone. Ky cannot find out that his mother will be behind her death."

"Interesting. This is getting better by the minute. Well, now, let's go check out the Nibus I would love to see the work they have done."

They proceeded to the laboratory, looking through the window. They saw what was left of Logan. Gruesomely torn apart and watching the creatures feast on his blood. They also noticed what was left of the remains of Enid in the far back corner of the room. One of the creatures arched back, giving a hideous scream as though it wanted more.

"Ahh, yes. This, I believe, is the greatest creations I have made. You are a genius, Milledge, to have thought of combining your DNA with the mixture of the DNA samples I provided. This is fantastic! Let us go celebrate at Millicent's pub and play some Dilent!"

"Shall we?" Milledge smiled in delight as he motioned to the doorway leading out from the laboratory.

Chapter 16

It was morning. It was so wonderful being back in Ky's arms again. He moved some of his belongings into my chamber. He said he could not stand sleeping alone without me not there knowing I am finally where I belong. I have never felt so alive, so happy. Waking up next to him was the greatest feeling of all.

There was pounding on the door. I quickly got out of bed. Ky groggy, grabbing my arm letting his hand slide down to mine while I was getting up. He smiled at me and winked, and let go of me.

I answered the door. It was Alex and Nikki. Worried, as they had not seen Logan since arriving at the palace.

"It's not like him to just ignore me. Something isn't right, Jay." Alex pleaded.

"Maybe he just needs some time, Alex. I mean, after all, everything that has happened and he knows I am not coming back to him."

"No, Jay. Even in his most dire times, he always goes to Alex no matter what. He would have somehow left a note or something if he wanted to be by himself. Something seems fishy. I don't know what. I saw the Queen, Ky's mother, she seems a bit off. That Milledge guy, well there is something about him I don't like. He seems very shady." Nikki stated.

"First of all, Nikki, Ky is here, so please do not speak of his mother like that. Second of all, I thought Milledge was very nice. We had a nice long conversation yesterday. I somewhat consider him a friend."

Nikki whispered, "And your thoughts on his mother? You didn't say anything, so I think you kinda feel the same as I do."

"Nikki, I am not going to discuss this, not right now."

"Morning Nikki, Alex." Ky said, nodding to them as he entered the room.

"Morning." They both said in sequence.

"What are you discussing?" Ky asked.

"Logan is missing." Alex stated.

"I am sure he is taking time letting everything sink in, knowing Jaycenda is now with me."

"As we were explaining to Jay, this is not like Logan not to keep in contact. When he has problems, he always comes to me, no matter what. This is not like him. We have been best friends for a very long time; I know him a lot better than you, Ky!" Alex said in anger.

"Alright, well then. I'll have Milledge assist you both to his chambers see if he is in there. If not, we can see about getting some people out looking for him.”

“Good. At least something will be done.” Alex said, giving Nikki a worried look.

Milledge came to my chamber and all of us went with him to Logan’s. Sure enough, he was nowhere to be found. Nothing left behind, nothing stating he was going exploring. Alex was right this is not like him. Now that I am the High Queen against my wishes, I had called upon a search for him. There had been nothing. There are over two hundred thousand people in Atlantis. He could be anywhere.

“Thank you for sending out a search for him, Jay. I know you two had your problems, but at least you care enough to make sure he is safe.” Nikki stated.

“Nikki, I would do the same thing for anyone. Let’s not try to get ahead of ourselves, though, and he may be somewhere in Atlantis that we just don’t know about.”

“This is true.”

I found Dad and Mom and filled them in on the events. Mom noticed the necklace was now on me. She was surprised no announcement had been made that I was now the High Queen. She had stated that it is always announced once the necklace had chosen.

I explained to mom my feelings toward Helena. Mom did not know what to make of it as they had been dear friends for such a long time.

"I do not understand. Why had she not made the announcement? You are now the High Queen. This is not like her. I need to go to my chamber and relax see if I can get a vision." She said as she hugged me goodbye.

Ky had gone out with Milledge to look for Logan, and I needed to go to my chamber. I had an urge to lay down. As I started to go to the bed, I was becoming light-headed. As I lay down, I closed my eyes. I started feeling cool and was concentrating. I wanted a vision. Something was not right; I could feel it.

I saw Logan pacing back and forth I saw him talking to someone, but it was like he was talking to me. It was like I was looking through someone else's eyes. He was saying how much he really did love me and wanted me back and that I belonged to him. Then he disappeared. I then saw a war: creatures battling creatures. Most of the creatures were mythological, ones you read about in ancient Greek. There were centaurs, mermaids, harpies. I saw myself riding Pegasus and using some of my abilities. I saw myself healing Ky. I saw the death of Nikki and Alex, I could not prevent it. I saw most of Atlantis destroyed. I saw us being on a losing end, and then I saw myself going into the labyrinth and releasing the Minotaurs that could possibly help us. I saw Helena frightened, trying to destroy me, but then I saw Ky protecting me from her. I saw an elder also with great powers; I did not know whose side she was on. Then I woke up. I did not want to think about it. My heartbeat raced, and I was sweating. I needed to go find Mom and let her know of this vision. I was frightened. I needed to find a way to protect Nikki and Alex, but from what I saw, there was no possible way. I saw nothing of Dad, Mom or Trish, so I have no idea what lies in their future. I did not even see my own. What this means, I do not know. But I know I am now the High Queen, and I need to protect my people.

I had a knock on the door right when I was getting ready to look for Mom. It was Asher and Arileen; they were the twin seers. I invited them in. Both were average height with sandy brown hair and crystal blue eyes like Mom and me. They explained to me that since I am now the High Queen, they were to come to me with any visions they may have had. They advised me they had told Helena of their vision a few months ago when Ky and my mom were visiting me that they had seen some horrible things and advised Helena to have splicing engineers create centaurs, mermaids, harpies, and Pegasus. This made sense with what I had seen. They stated they had a vision all would be lost if nothing had been done. They stated that they had a feeling to keep the secrecy away from the head engineer Dylian, as to why, they were not sure. His access to part of the laboratories had been denied to keep the secrecy. They shared their recent vision with me. They have the same vision; one may vary little details, but more or less, it is the same. Their vision was very similar to the one I had just had. I could not think. Something big was about to happen, and the problem was we did not know when. I questioned them about this elder I had seen that had powers as well. They had advised me it was Millicent, Milledge's aunt. They, as well could not tell which side she was on. We were trying to figure out what exactly was going on. I advised them of the horrible creatures I had seen that the mythological creatures were fighting. I told them how the skin was black as night looked as though it could not be penetrated. Skull oblong, large white eyes, no nose or ears. Large wings that spread out like a bat, slithered tongues, cobra hoods, fangs, claws that looked like they could rip through anything, and talons. I saw them scaling walls, flying, and swimming underwater. I also shared my vision of them standing upright like a man and muscular. I had no idea what this meant.

They advised they had not seen these creatures; they had seen the war and the creatures they had suggested being created fighting for us. I did not disclose my vision of Ky's mother trying to kill me. I do not know if they had that same vision and did not want to tell me. They had left my chamber, and Mom came rushing in.

Chapter 17

It has been over a week. Milledge was growing weary of tagging along for this fake search when he already knew the truth. Logan was long gone, and no one would know. He excused himself away and made his way to the Artilla Gardens. He noticed Trish sitting on a bench whimpering, knees propped up to her chest. She was beautiful, he thought to himself.

"My dear, are you alright?"

Sniffling and letting the tears roll down her cheeks, she responded. "No. The man I had fallen in love with is with another woman. I have loved him for months, and he chose her."

"Who may this be?"

"Sam. I had tried everything I could to get him to be with me, but he only had eyes for her. He said he had always loved her and knew they would be together again someday. I tried to tell him I was here, she wasn't, and that I loved him and had for some time now. He said he only considered us as friends, and it could never be anything more than that. We were together a few times, but he felt so guilty he did not want to continue being intimate with me. He said it was not right. He was in love with someone else, the mother of his daughter. He said someday she would be coming back, and they would be together, and he didn't mean to get my hopes up. I just never thought that it would actually happen."

"Trish, from our small talks, you are a very intelligent woman. And you are very beautiful; looking at you, you take my breath away. You do not deserve that. You deserve better and deserve to be loved."

"Thank you, Milledge. I sometimes wonder if I was meant to be alone. I have had my share of love interests but had only truly been in love once, and well, as you know, he did not choose me. I feel as though there is something completely wrong with me. I know I am beautiful, I am a nice person, and I do things for others, but I seem not to get anything in return. All my family and friends are gone; since we have been here, Sam hasn't really spoken to me. I feel all alone. Maybe that's what I am supposed to be alone."

Milledge sat down beside her, and he cupped her face. "No, you were not meant to be alone. No one is meant to be alone. Sam is obviously a fool. You deserve more than that." He then brushed her hair behind her ear and kissed her gently.

She reciprocated his kiss.

"Thank you, Milledge. That was nice."

"It was my pleasure. I would love to get to know you more Trish. You are so beautiful and sweet, and you don't even know it."

"I would love to take you up on that offer." She said with a smile.

They headed to the pub. He introduced her to Millicent. She provided them with some ale, and he showed her how to play Dilent.

"Ok, so I take these darts that you call a quiber and try to hit that moving dot, and each time I hit it, it speeds up?"

"Indeed," he said, reaching the three quibers on the table while looking at her smiling.

Trish gave it a whirl; she found it to be a lot of fun. She was enjoying her time with Milledge. He was a lot different than what she had expected. They spent several hours together before retiring to his chamber.

The next morning, Trish had awoken. Milledge was already up watching her sleep.

"Good morning, beautiful."

"Good morning." She said smiling at him.

"That was a wonderful night we shared. And I hope we have many more. There is something about you. I do not know what it is, but I like it. Sam is a fool. He has no idea what he has given up. Then again, maybe I should thank him?"

She laughed. "Milledge, I should be the one thanking you! You made me realize I don't have to be all alone. At least there is a chance for me." She laughed again.

"Be with me Trish."

"Yes."

"Would you be with me no matter what?"

"Yes."

"Even if you knew I wanted to take over Atlantis and the world?"

"Yes. Milledge, there is something about you as well. I cannot put my finger on it, but you have helped me immensely get over Sam. And I thank you for that. I see myself with you."

"Good. You mustn't say anything to anyone about my wanting to take over. I was being serious."

"And I was serious when I told you yes."

"So if I told you I haven't exactly been good; would you still want to be with me?"

"Yes. What is it you have done?"

"How do I know I can trust you?"

"You can trust me, and I have no one else."

"That Logan, well, let's just say he did not go exploring or anything. I pretty much disposed of him. I felt he might get into the way of things. And once I take over Atlantis, you will be my Queen."

"You killed Logan?"

"I did."

"Because you thought he was going to get into the way of things?"

"Yes. See, he wanted Jaycenda back. Well, she, from what I hear, is the High Queen."

"Huh? How is Sam's daughter the High Queen?"

"She was born with a "mark" that automatically made her the High Queen. I did not care for him, and with his whining about getting her back, I felt as though he would get in the way. He needed to be rid of. I thought maybe no one would notice his disappearance but I had been wrong. So, my plans are going to have to go into play quicker than expected. Helena has told me she did not want to give up being the High Queen. Jaycenda is the chosen one, and nothing can be done about that. Jaycenda needs to be taken out; Helena thinks once that is done, she will take her spot back. Well, my plan is to destroy her and her family as well. I have royal blood in me. Before Atlantis went under, my ancestors were the royals. Cyrus wanted to control the world and was succeeding. Then Arcadian, who had hidden the "mark," came forth announcing he was the true heir. Arcadian was ashamed of what Cyrus was doing; he had him destroyed, and his followers banished. He then somehow created the dome over Atlantis that you had seen when you first got here and, of course, sunk Atlantis to the bottom of the Abyss. So I figured to kill Jaycenda, Helena, and the rest of the royals I would anoint myself king. It is my right. I will need a Queen, and I choose you."

"Wow. I am at a loss for words. I will say this, Milledge. I will stand by your side no matter what may occur." She said smiling at him.

He smiled back; they continued the talk of him taking over and what his plans were. He was quickly falling for this woman. He had never fallen for anyone so quickly, not even with Enid. There was something about her, and he loved the fact he could share his secrets with her.

Chapter 18

I could not tell Ky about his mother. I could not hurt him like that, let alone have him be mad at me. Mom had a similar vision to what Asher, Arileen and I have had. This did not make any sense. Who would want to create this war that was going to happen? Was Helena behind it? But that did not make sense as she had heeded the advice of the twin seers. I did not understand anything that was going on. I thought I would take it upon myself to enter the labyrinth. Mom had told me that only the chosen who wears the necklace can enter unless you are accompanied by the chosen one. She said the Minotaurs obey the one who has the charm. I was not so much nervous about them as I knew my powers were growing more and more. I did not feel like walking to the entrance of the labyrinth, so I willed myself there.

The golden doorway was huge, and the etchings of the Minotaurs on it were frightening, but it did not scare me so easily. I had seen worse in my vision, and I believe they would be on my side.

I entered the doorway, and the charm started to glow. I could see several feet in front of me. But this was not enough light for me; it was too dark. I willed the bluish fire, and there I was also aglow. I heard the most horrible noises and growls but saw nothing. Where are they hiding? I was wandering around in circles, it seemed like. I went down staircases and pathways that led to dead ends. I wanted to cry I had no idea where I was. I then saw four beings start to come toward me. I could not make them out until they stepped further into the light. They all were scary-looking half man, half bull, very huge, and wearing a leather-like kilt. Each had a strap across their chest, wearing their strange weapons on their back. One carried what looked to be a sledgehammer, another an axe, another with a spear, and the fourth one-two swords that looked like a hook on the end of them. They each got down on one knee, placed their right arm against their chest, and bowed their heads. As though they knew I was now the chosen one and was serving me. I was not scared by them. Others would be.

"Please stand."

They had all stood. I introduced myself although they did not speak, they understood. I asked them to help me get to the crystal mom had told me about. They lead me down stairs and corridors, many twists and turns. I never thought I would ever be in this situation I was in. Nothing seemed to make sense to me anymore except for Ky.

There it was, the diamond-shaped crystal in the middle of the room. From floor to ceiling, casting a yellow glow. I still had the blue fire surrounding me, and I was not sure whether to stop it or not. I figured I would keep it going just to see what happened. I willed myself in front of the crystal. I looked at the Minotaurs; they were looking at me intensely and eagerly.

I placed my hand on the crystal; my hair was flying back like a gust of wind was coming from it; the fire coming from me continued. I closed my eyes.

I saw the past, I saw the present, and I saw the future. Who would have thought Atlanteans were originally from Mars? I mean, yeah, there had been speculation if there had once been life on Mars, but the crystal proved the theory was correct. As I gathered all that I could, I was receiving some type of directions to somewhere not in this universe. I did not understand any of this. Then, I felt a burst of energy so strong that I placed my other hand on the crystal; the energy grew stronger, and it was painful. I was screaming, and the Minotaurs were making noises that seemed more like a howling. I could tell they were spread out in the room. Circling the crystal by the noises they were making. The energy continued to flow through me; it was so strong I felt as though I could no longer stand. A few minutes later, I was pushed back from the crystal. I opened my eyes and looked at the crystal; it no longer had the glow. It looked just as though a plain crystal. I felt more alive than I already had with Ky. I had drained the crystal; I had all the knowledge it provided. I also felt as though my powers had grown. The Minotaurs came over and did their bow thing. I told them to rise. I learned of their names. The one with the sledgehammer was Bane. The one with the axe was

Axel. The one with the Spear was called Pike, and the last one Makeo. None have heard their names being called for thousands of years. That will change. They are living beings, after all. I had advised them of a vision I had and asked if they were to be on my side; they nodded and seemed to be giddy that they would be able to leave the labyrinth at some point to assist with helping Atlantis.

They assisted me back to the entrance and I willed myself to my chamber. Mom and Ky were sitting and talking about her vision. She had come over to me; she could tell I was starting to feel faint.

"What happened?" She asked.

I went into detail with Mom about everything and what had happened in the Labyrinth. Ky was in awe as he overheard us going over our visions again and overheard us whispering about his mother planning to destroy me. He stepped in.

"What do you mean my mother is planning to kill you?"

"I do not know the details as to why Ky; I have seen it and well as Jaycenda. It hurts me to have seen this, as I have known her for so long. We did not want to say anything to protect you. I know you love my daughter, and she loves you; that is why we said nothing. We did not mean for you to overhear. Please understand we do not wish to come between you and your mother." Luciana told him with a saddened face.

"It already has. Jaycenda, sweetie, I do not plan to go anywhere." He said to me, cupping my face with both hands and looking me in the eye. "I love you, I chose you, and I will do my best to protect you."

Tears roll down my cheeks. He truly loves me deeply, and I love him deeply.

"Ky my love. Something happens to you, and I don't know exactly what, but I had seen myself healing you and your mother then coming after me and you trying to protect me from her. Nikki and Alex are killed. I only saw their bodies. I don't know what to make of things. All we know is there is going to be a war, and possibly soon."

"My mother will not hurt you. This I vow: if I have to stop her myself, I will. She may be my mother, and I do love her, but she will not take my soul mate away from me. If you were to die, I would die with you. You have my heart, and you are my everything. I love you!" He then kissed me passionately. Mom excused herself, wanting to give us some alone time and to spend time with Sam.

Ky picked me up and carried me into the bedroom. We made passionate love practically all night. I could not imagine my world without him in it.

The next morning, I could tell something was not right. Could this be the day? Or something to do with the energy I drained from the crystal? I cannot explain the feelings I was having. Everything seemed to be more intense since I had drained the crystal. I could feel the energy flowing inside me.

Nikki and Alex came to visit, still worried about Logan. I simply told them he was still being searched for. I had advised them to prepare for a war. I did not want to disclose the vision of their death. I wanted to embrace every moment I could spend with them and reminisce on the times before the events happened. Ky had left the chamber; he would not disclose where he was going. I was praying he was not going to confront his mother.

Chapter 19

"Mother, we need to talk!"

"Ky my son, how are you? I have not seen much of you lately since that girl has been here. It has been what three months now?"

"What are you planning, mother?" Ky demanded.

"What are you talking about, Ky? I have no plans for anything."

"There have been more than one vision of you. Trying to kill Jaycenda! Do not do it Mother! I love her! She is my soulmate. I will do what I must do to protect her!"

"Ky, I would do no such thing! I like the girl. She suits you, and I see she makes you happy." She said to him as she turned her back toward him, concerned the seers know and how she could try to fix things with her son.

"Are you jealous that she is the chosen one? And is now the High Queen?"

"Jealous of her being the chosen one? No. Of her now being the High Queen. Humph, I guess you could say I am, as I have ruled for many years, and she knows nothing about being a leader!"

"And she had even told you she did not want it, even though she is the CHOSEN ONE! There is nothing to be jealous about! So what you ruled for years. Sit back and enjoy being free from your duties! I'm with her, and I will do whatever it is I have to do to protect her!" Ky yelled at his mother, hurriedly left her chamber, and made his way back to Jaycenda.

He could tell by the look on his mother's face the visions were going to be true. He was full of anger. He ran into Asher and Arileen. He discussed the visions Jaycenda and Luciana had.

"I know you are only permitted to discuss your visions with the High Queen. A lot is at stake. I love Jaycenda, and I want nothing more than to protect her. I ask of you, if you had foreseen anything more, to please share them with me. I know of what is to happen with the war."

Asher spoke, "Yes Ky. We have had another vision, and it is not good. We were hoping this vision of the war would give us time to prepare; however, it starts today. We were hoping for some time, but there is no time left. It will be later today. We need permission to go to the laboratories and speak with Landry. Your mother did order us to have him start splicing and creating the creatures of years past that we saw in our visions. They need to get them prepped and ready to go."

"Yes, go to him, have him release them, get them prepared! If he has any questions, you tell him the orders came from Jaycenda. Time is running short; hurry now!" He said as he started making his way back to Jaycenda's chamber. The twins took off running, hoping they would make it there without any trouble.

"Jaycenda?"

"Yes Ky?" I asked as he ran over to me hugging me and kissing me.

"Whatever happens, know that I love you very, very much!" He kissed me and hugged me again.

"Ky, what is wrong? You are pale and sweaty."

"I spoke with mother. She said she has no intentions of harming you. However, what disturbed me the most was the look on her face; I knew she was not telling me the truth. I then came across the twin seers. Jaycenda, sweetie, it's starting today. They saw the war happening today!" He said squeezing me.

Dad, Mom, Nikki, and Alex all came over to us; we were all hugging each other and letting each other know how much we loved each other not knowing what may lay ahead.

I have had a feeling since I woke up that something was not right about today. I did not know what it had to do with, but now I know. I am scared for all of us. I do not know if I should make any type of announcement to the people. I just don't know.

"If you announce it to the people, there will be frantic, possibly an uprise. It may even cause for the war to start earlier." Mom stated.

"You are right; we cannot have chaos before the war. I just do not know what to do." I said, cradling my stomach. I was hiding the fact that I thought I might be pregnant. I am conflicting on saying anything.

"I had Arileen and Asher rush off to Landry to get prepared and release the centaurs, harpies, and whatever else they had foreseen he and Fiona created. I told them to tell Landry the orders came directly from you." Ky stated with concern.

"Thank you, Ky, for believing everything we have been seeing. I love you."

"I love you too."

"There is something I need to tell all of you. I must go into this battle; I have foreseen it. What my outcome is, I do not know. However…" I trailed off. I was choking about to tell them. "I think I may be pregnant."

"You will not go off into battle, Jay!" Dad demanded. "And how so quickly would you know?"

"We Atlanteans do know quickly, Sam; remember, it was just a few days we were together. I knew I was with our daughter."

"Ok, yeah point taken," Dad said.

"Jaycenda, I will marry you when we come out of this. I do not want you going into battle, not with carrying our child." He told me, placing his hand on my stomach and rubbing it back and forth. "We will get through this."

"Ky, I know what you are saying, but I have no choice; I must enter this battle. I must protect who I can. Our people count on us to keep them safe, and that is what I plan to do."

We were all hugging each other, and Ky and I were receiving congratulations. Asher and Arileen knocked on the door.

"It is done. Landry had already let the mermaids loose. The centaurs were talking amongst themselves and choosing their weapons, Pegasus had already been developed and been in a stall. The harpies Landry said he does not want to release just yet, as they are full of rage." Arileen mentioned.

"Time is running short; let us start preparing," Luciana advised.

Chapter 20

Milledge stood in the courtyard. The thunderstorm rolled in fierce and hard. Day turned to night and lightening was streaking the darkened sky. Milledge loved this; this was the perfect day to release his creations. The thunder grew louder. It started to pour. Milledge allowed himself to get soaked, looking into the sky, watching the lightning dance, and hearing the thunder roaring and the waves of the ocean crashing against the walls of Atlantis.

He started to smile with the look of evil in his eye. Today is definitely the day. Milledge turned around and went back into the palace.

Milledge made his way back to the chamber. The storm was a turn-on for him; he took Trish once more as soon as he got back to the chamber.

"That was wonderful. Love." She said with a smile.

"You have no idea how much you have been on my mind. I need you to stay in the chamber and keep the door locked. I am going to release my creatures. And soon Atlantis will be ours." He said with a smirk.

"I will stay here until you come back."

"Do so. Dylian will be coming soon."

"I will."

Dylian came quickly. He and Milldege went to their laboratory. Milledge advised Dylian that he was going to open the stone doorway beneath them to set them free. It led into the waterways of the moats. He knew these creatures would be able to swim and knew the chamber would flood giving them the access needed.

Milledge pulled the screen up; they were watching as the Nibus were starting to get ready to fight each other. He pushed a button they felt the door move below them. Water started to gush into the room. The creatures were anxiously going against the currents, trying to push them back. They fought against it and went underwater and out into the moats.

Dylian was delighted. He was hoping once Milledge took over Atlantis he would be right by his side, as part of the royal court. This Milledge knew but led Dylian to believe he would let him rule alongside him. Although he appreciated Dylian's help, he was no longer needed. Milledge walked with Dylian near the table he used to have Enid restrained. He gave Dylian a few quick blows to the head, placed him on the table, and put the crystal restraints on. Dylian came to a few minutes later, questioning Milledge as to why he did this.

"Well it's simple Dylian. When all is done there will be one ruler-ME! I needed your assistance to get the splicing done. I have no more use for you now."

Milledge forced Dylian's mouth open and, forced a silver ball into his mouth, and forced him to swallow it. Dylian's eyes grew wide as whatever he had swallowed opened inside him, tearing him from inside, and he started to choke on his own blood.

Milledge always seemed to be pleased with his inventions. He wanted to go see what the damages are going on now.

He had forewarned Millicent of what was to come. He did not like the look she was giving him about it. She felt he should not go that length, and much of Atlantis was destroyed. He did not want to hear of it. He did have her do a casting for the creatures to avoid attacking him, as they did have part of him in them.

Milledge told Trish once more not to leave the chamber and to keep it locked while he went to check on things. He stepped out onto the cliff side, watching fires ablaze, his creatures scaling buildings and flying about, killing one person after another. He heard a horn in the distance. He looked over into the direction it was coming from. He saw several centaurs coming out to play. He heard a beautiful song coming from the moat below. As he looked down he could see several women swimming in the moat.

One of the Nibus was drawn to the vibrations of the singing. It flew over above where they were. One of the mermaids jumped out of the water, grabbing onto it, sinking her sharp teeth into the Nibus, and splashing back down into the water, carrying it under.

The other mermaids went down below to assist. Milledge was curious about this. What mermaid has fangs and horns? Not anything from what he remembered hearing about.

He then heard a loud splash; the Nibus came out of the water, hovering with the mermaid, ripping her in half, throwing her back down into the water, and flying back toward the city.

Milledge was proud. He had outdone himself this time. These were his children. Atlantis was surely nothing like what it once had been. He continued watching as the centaurs went into battle. They were tough, alright, but were not enough to defeat his creatures. He heard something land behind him, and it was one of the Nibus. It sensed with its forked tongue and had left him alone. It started to make its way into the palace.

He followed, wanting to make sure his newfound love was going to be safe. He watched as Marcade was coming down the marbled stairway; it flew over, grabbing him and ripping him to shreds. Alex was walking down the hallway and witnessed the killing; he started running back down the hall; the creature saw him and went flying down the hallway after him, pushing him from behind onto the ground; it was hissing. Alex turned around and tried to fight it off with all of his might and tried to use some of his wrestling moves on it. It was too strong. Its cobra hood opened, and it spewed the plasma saliva on his face, paralyzing him. It took its claws and tore into his chest and stomach. Draining him of his blood.

Chapter 21

"NOOOOOOOOO!!!" I cried out. I knew. Alex was gone everyone was rushing over to me.

"Jay? What's wrong?" Nikki asked.

"Nikki. I'm so sorry!" I cried. "It has started. Alex is gone. I felt it, and I saw it happening."

"No, Jay. He is alright; he just went to our chamber to get something. Nothing has happened. He will be back."

"Nikki, maybe she is right. She had drained the energy from the crystal, and her powers had grown. I hate to even think that, but we need to face reality." Dad said to her, hugging her.

She pulled away. She came over and gave me a hug.

"I won't believe it Jay. I love you, and you are my best friend but I will not believe Alex is gone."

"Nikki, I did not want to tell you this, but I saw in a previous vision you were both gone. Nothing I could do to save you; please do not go after him. If I could not save him, at least let me try to save you!"

"You mean to tell me you had a vision that we were dead, and you said nothing! I cannot believe you have kept that from us! He is fine, and I am going to go catch up to him!"

"Nikki please don't!" I was upset with myself. I should have said something; this was killing me.

Nikki left my chamber I went after her. Ky tried to hold me back, but I let go and continued after her. Ky came running after me, as well as Mom and Dad.

Nikki was going down the hallway when she noticed the creature overtop of Alex drinking his blood. She let out a loud, horrifying scream. I was right behind her. It rose up and started coming toward her. I quickly got infront of her. Anger and instinct was kicking in. Pushed my arms out back and forth, having balls of fire protruding from my hands toward the being. It was backing away toward the entrance as I kept walking toward it. It had left the palace.

"I'm so sorry Nikki."

She cried as she went over, clutching Alex's body. "Why? Why did it have to be like this?" She cried out.

"Alex. Oh Alex. I love you. Please remember that." She was shaking, and she was in shock.

"I want everyone back to the chamber. I am going to let the Minotaurs free."

"Jaycenda, we are going to attempt to have Landry set the harpies free if we can make it. We had seen them in our vision, so I assumed we would get there safely. Be safe all of you." Asher said to all of us.

"And you as well, both of you. Safe travels. Hopefully, our paths will meet again." I told the twins.

Everyone else was back in the chamber. Ky wanted to come with me, I told him I needed to do this by myself. He hugged me and wished for my safe return.

Mom and Dad went over to Nikki to be by her side. She was at a loss and starting to hyperventilate.

I willed myself to the entrance of the labyrinth. I entered, and the charm was glowing again. I had to use the blue firepower I had again, like the last time. I had called out to the Minotaurs they came rushing to me. I advised them that the only creatures they were to go after were the black creatures. I described what they looked like to them. Bane threw his head back and beat his chest like a gorilla would do. It seemed as though he was anxious. They were under my control; they knew what they had to do. They ran out the entrance and into the palace. I willed myself back to the chamber.

Mom and Dad were still comforting Nikki.

"Where is Ky?" I asked worriedly.

"We could not stop him, Jay. He said he was going after his mother; he believed she was behind all of this."

I tried to see if I could somehow locate him in the palace as the balls of fire were a new surprise power that was done on instinct. I concentrated, and I then felt as though he was in the throne room. I willed myself there.

Ky was arguing with his mother, asking her why she had created this war that was going on outside the palace. She insisted she had nothing to do with it. He insisted she had. He was telling her he knew she was behind it as she wanted me dead.

They continued to argue. He told her I was carrying his child. She grew very angry with everything he was telling her and the fact that I was pregnant; she could not stop herself; she pulled a knife from behind her dress. I screamed as she lunged it into his stomach.

She saw what she had done, backed away, asking herself what she had done, and crying. I went running over to Ky, crying.

"No, Ky, you are not going to leave me! You hear me! You will not leave me!" I yelled at him and kissed him. He was not responding. I placed my hand over the wound, wanting to heal him like I had healed Dad when I had burned him by accident. I concentrated enough the yellow glow was bright for a few seconds.

The yellow light from my hand over his wound now faded. He slowly opened his eyes and smiled. "Thank you for saving me."

"You! You made me do this to my son! You will pay for

that!" Helena screamed in anger, her hair a mess.

I used some of my power to push her back across the room, but I was growing weak. I had already used a good bit of my powers to teleport and use the fireballs and the blue fire. I was not sure how much more I could use.

She got up. She still had the knife in her hand.

"Jay, my love, remember I told you I would do what it takes to protect you?"

"Yes, I do."

"I am honoring my word." He got up and went running toward his mother. He speared into her, knocking her onto the floor and the knife flying across the room. As she was getting up, he did a roundhouse kick on her.

"Sorry Mother. You planned to try to kill the love of my life, you try to kill me, and you started whatever is going on outside the palace walls. I will protect her until I die. And today will not be that day!" He grabbed her, put her in a headlock, and snapped her neck.

I never expected Ky to kill his own mother, not even to protect me. He had, though, and I could not imagine what was going through his head right now. He gently laid her down and started to cry and ask for forgiveness. I went to comfort him.

As the tears rolled down his cheeks, he grabbed onto me,

holding me. "I swore I would protect you no matter what. I love you."

I had no words. I just witnessed my love kill his own mother. I willed us back to the chamber.

Mom asked what happened and explained everything to her what happened. She was in shock. She knew how much Helena loved Ky and was stunned that she had tried to kill him.

Had I not been there, I don't know If he would have made it. She punctured it in pretty deep.

"I cannot thank you enough for being there when you were." Ky said.

Nikki was in a daze. I had never seen her like this. She would not speak to anyone or look at anyone. I can understand that, had Ky been gone, I would probably be feeling the same as she was. It was a close call. I knew there was not anything I could do to save Alex. He had lost so much blood. I kept looking back on my vision. I think I have changed my path. When I saw Alex and Nikki dead, they were lying together. She is still here. Had I changed the course and saved Nikki by going after her? I questioned Mom about this. She said it was very possible visions could be changed.

"I know I feel drained, but I need to get out there. I need to save our people."

"Please, Jay, stay here where it is safe." Ky begged.

"Ky, she will be fine. I had seen this. We need to stay here. Let her go and do what she needs to do." Luciana advised.

Ky looked at me, saddened that I was leaving. "Promise me you will stay safe and keep our baby safe."

"I will Ky. I swear. I love you too much to let go." I said, kissing him goodbye.

I felt the urge to go to the courtyard. I had to stop once at the courtyard. I was having a vision. Most of Atlantis was destroyed, and not many survivors from the aftermath. The Minotaurs were our protectors; it seemed as though they were the only things that could kill these creatures. There were two centaurs that survived. It seemed as though all the hard work was put into making the small armies to help us were not very useful but helped as much as possible to keep Atlantis alive. I saw I was standing in the circle of the throne room again and saw a huge bright light coming from the floor and people stepping through the light. I did not understand this. At least not yet; I did not have time to figure it out.

I looked up in the sky, hearing screeches and growling. I was watching those creatures taking down the harpies. You could hear the harpies being tortured and in pain.

Pegasus was in the courtyard as though it was waiting for

me. As I approached him, one of the creatures and a harpy came tumbling down from the sky, crashing onto the cobblestone and rolling around, trying to kill each other. The harpy looked over at me briefly before concentrating back on the creature, as though it had been in pain, half bird half human female from the torso up, both having arms and wings; it had been trying to get the creature off it, their talons still locked. I saw the black creature produce the cobra head and spew something on the harpy. The harpy stopped moving. You could see it was still breathing. The creature raised its claws. I threw my arm out toward it; it was as though a lightning bolt had hit it. It back away from the harpy. It started to come toward me. I started to use the fireballs on it like I did earlier; it took off flying back toward the city.

Chapter 22

As weary as I was growing, I needed to try to stop all this destruction. I hopped on Pegasus. He took off running to the cliff and spread his wings. Flying over Atlantis and seeing the horror the city had become. You could smell the death in the air. Buildings burning and the Artilla Gardens, where Ky and I had watched our first sunset in Atlantis now gone. I could not believe this. It was so unbelievable this was happening. I could hear the screams of people all over. I had Pegasus fly over the palace.

Milledge was standing there in front of one of those creatures, smiling and looking as though he was talking to it, and it was obeying. Ky's mom was right, and she did not have anything to do with this. I cannot tell Ky, and he would only be in more pain knowing he killed his mother partly because of something he thought she was a part of. I couldn't. As I watched, two Minotaurs went running over toward the creature. Milledge tried to stop them, only to be pushed heavily off to the side. The creature was trying to take on two Minotaurs. They were much bigger and stronger looking than the Nibus. Milldege tried to stop the Minotaurs again, and again only to be pushed back down hard. They were listening to me; they were not attacking Milledge, only these creatures.

The creature spread its wings, and Axel came running with his battle axe. It had some type of metal I had never seen before. He extended the handle with a jerk, went running toward it so fast, and slashed its wings off. The thing let out a blood-curdling scream. Bane then came running with his sledgehammer he gave it a swing, and spikes appeared coming out from it. He started to run toward it. The creature opened its cobra hood and spewed the saliva on the Bane. It didn't affect him. Bane took his weapon, slashing into the cobra's hood; the spikes penetrated the side of this creature's head. It fell to the ground, letting out a loud screeching scream. The Minotaurs were trying to tear the thing apart but were having difficulty. Makeo then came running over. He had the two hooked swords.

As the creature was lying face down on the ground, the two Minotaurs there were each pulling on an arm. Makeo placed his right foot on the back of the creature. He then evenly punctured each eye with the swords. The creature yelled even louder when he did that and began to pull the head back with all his might. Still alive and screaming an awful sound, Pike came running. He had the spear; he gave it a jerk and small additional spikes came out along the sides of the spear nearly halfway down the spear. Running, then jumped in the air, bringing the spear directly through the head of the creature. I do believe this thing was dead for sure.

Milledge got up screaming that one of his creatures was dead and that this was impossible; this shouldn't be. I had Pegasus fly down. He trotted toward the Minotaurs when he landed.

"Milledge, this is your doing?"

"Child, you have no idea how long and hard I have worked on this day, and you are ruining it for me."

"This is all you. I do not understand. Ky killed his mother thinking she was behind it besides trying to kill me."

Milledge had an evil laugh. "Oh, she planned on killing you, alright. She wanted her spot back. But she didn't know I had planned on taking the rest of the royals out to have my rightful place on the throne. You ruined everything."

"Milledge, you had one of my best friends killed and Ky killing his mother. You have destroyed much of Atlantis due to your selfishness. Minotaurs, I know I said only the black creatures, but go on and have a little fun with Milledge." I said angrily.

The Minotaurs started to knock Milledge down. He kept trying to get back up. Pike broke Milledge's arm. Bane took his sledgehammer with the spikes on the end and plunged it into his back. Milledge screamed in agony, still alive, breathing heavily, begging for his life. He was on the ground face down. He thought things would be different. Had this been what Enid was really hiding from him and had asked him to change his way? Axel took his turn and stomped on Milledge's head. They heard the mermaids splashing around in the moat and they tossed Milledge over the cliff. The mermaids were having their turn at him.

All the harpies were dead, and I believe there had only been three. I saw two centaurs still hunting the creatures; they seemed to have been the last. I saw many centaurs lying around lifeless.

This was the most horrifying thing I have ever witnessed. My visions of destruction were nothing compared to this. I saw many people killed in the streets; some looked as though they may have been fighting alongside the centaurs.

I was keeping a lookout for the other creatures. I saw two other bodies, pretty much destroyed like the other. That's three down, two more to go. The Minotaurs must have been building up for this day for a very long time. As I rode Pegasus, I flew over where the airships were. There was the elder Millicent. She was destroying all the ships so no one could leave Atlantis. She was nearly done.

"Why are you destroying the ships? We need them to get out of Atlantis!" I yelled down to her.

"You! I watched you have my nephew killed! I was going to help you have Milledge stop this madness. But then you had him killed. So therefore no one will be leaving Atlantis unless it is by death!"

She was shooting some type of light at me. I put my arm up in defense and somehow created a shield. Well, this old woman wants to play games; then let's play games! Pegasus swooped down toward her. I was shooting the fireballs at her. She dodged each one. She tried to strike me again with her laser-like light. I teleported off Pegasus. I had willed myself to be hidden behind a destroyed ship.

"Oh, someone wants to be tricky, tricky. You are no match for this old mystic girl! I have lived much longer than you, by almost two hundred years. I have put in a lot of my time. Of course, we Atlanteans do live much longer than those pesky humans. Show yourself girl!"

I stayed put, trying to plan my next move. I was watching her while trying to remain hidden. She motioned her hand, moving debris, wondering where I was hiding.

I wish I could multiply myself to confuse her I knew that was one power I did not have. Two places at once that would be awesome. I had to think of the safety of the baby.

"Millicent, what are you doing? This was our only means to get off of Atlantis?" A young man said to her.

"Stay out of this Bray!"

"No! You destroyed pretty much all these ships. I have been watching you. Why? Because your nephew was killed? Look at what he had done!"

"You do not backtalk me, Bray!"

"I may be your apprentice, but I will tell you when you are wrong."

"Be off, boy. I am busy hunting for a pest."

"Well, here I am," I said as I willed myself from a distance off to the left of Bray.

"Oh look, and there she be!" She said with an evil smirk.

I became hotter and hotter, the blue fire protruding. I was furious, I never expected anything like this to happen, and this day seemed never ending.

The old woman looked at me dumbfounded. She held her arms up and pushed them toward me; a gust of wind blew against me heavily. We were going back and forth, using our powers toward one another. I was growing weaker. I had already used a lot of my power, and I could not use hardly anymore.

She cackled. "Is that all you got, girl? You are weak!"

I used the last of my energy to teleport behind her. I had a sharp piece of metal clutched in my hand. I stabbed her in the back with it. She slowly wobbled around in shock as to what had happened.

"You will pay for that!"

Bray stepped between us.

"You always said to do good, not evil. Everything you have told me tonight you have gone against. You will have to go through me to get to her." He pushed his arm out he started to do some enchanting. He lifted her off the ground. She was trying to fight back but couldn't. One of the last creatures left saw her in midair and grabbed her. She tried to use some of her powers against it, but she was too weak. It threw her down and then started to slash her and drain her blood. Three of the Minotaurs made their way over. They got ahold of it before it was able to take off. They destroyed it like the others.

"Thank you, Bray."

"You are welcome. I did not understand her desire behind destroying nearly of the ships. I guess we will never get out of Atlantis now that it has been destroyed."

"That's it!"

"What?"

"Bray try to gather all survivors. I drained the energy from the crystal, and I had been given directions to someplace, not in this universe. I then saw a vision of a bright light coming from the circle and people walking through it. Maybe that's it! Maybe that's the sign I was looking for. What if that is a portal to another place?"

"It would be possible." He said anxiously.

"Only one problem: there is one left of these creatures somewhere here; we cannot take any chances. I want it destroyed. It seems to be in hiding."

"Or maybe the Minotaurs had already destroyed it?"

"I will find out."

I called for one of them to come over. One approached me I asked if this was the last of those creatures; it had nodded at me, letting me know they had taken care of the other one.

This had been a long day. I headed back to the palace. Pegasus came back to get me and take me up. Bray was gathering the survivors and having them assist him in finding more.

When I got back to the chamber, everyone was hugging me. I had to lie down before anything more occurred.

I must have slept for hours. When I awoke, I felt so refreshed. I had to stretch. I got ready and went into the sitting room. I explained what I thought may take us to another place. Atlantis was practically non-livable now, and nearly all the ships destroyed. I told them about Bray coming in and somewhat saving the day and how he was looking for survivors to bring to the palace. He agreed that my theory may very well take us elsewhere.

"Well, Jay, let's go find out," Dad said anxiously.

Ky came from behind me, holding me and rubbing my belly. He then kissed me softly and whispered, "You know we will always be together."

I kissed him back, telling him I knew we would be.

Nikki was still in a state of shock and was not speaking. Mom had helped her up. All of us went toward the throne room, stopping at the top of the stairway in front of the doorway. Bray was having the survivors come into the palace. Some were mumbling they didn't care how bad it was they did not want to leave. It was their choice. I stood at the top of the stairway and spoke to the large, crowded foyer. Trish had left Milledge's chamber and joined the crowd, not understanding what was happening.

"My people. This day has been truly horrifying. Words cannot describe how awful I feel. Atlantis has been pretty much destroyed. We have lost many. We lost Helena, Marcade, Milledge, Alex, and many more thousands of people. We have a chance at a new way of life, if you would like to start fresh, then join us or choose to stay here where there is not much to rebuild. That choice I am leaving up to you."

The Minotaurs made their way to the top of the stairs. Jaycenda proceeded to explain that the Minotaurs had saved them from being destroyed. They were their protectors.

Trish was trying to sink this all in. Milledge was supposed to come back for her, but now that it seems like everything is over and Milledge had lost. She was beside herself. She felt all alone all over again. She blamed Jaycenda. She would follow her to this new place she was talking about, and when the time was right, she would get her revenge.

Jaycenda had the Minotaurs go into the throne room and remove Helena's body off to the dining hall that was right off from the throne room. She did not want anyone to get upset seeing her lay there lifeless, let alone have Ky see and have him relive it all over again.

Jaycenda then went into the throne room. She went into the middle of the circle as she had done so before. The energy was great; she was remembering what the crystal had given to her to guide her. She threw her arms up in the air and felt a wind gust coming from the floor and the light she saw in her vision. She started talking in another tongue that was different from the last time. She now needed to step out of the circle after her chanting.

The light was more or less a huge portal, a doorway, so to speak. Ky stood beside me. There may have been at least one hundred survivors who wanted to see if there was a better place than what was left of Atlantis. The rest of the survivors wanted to remain and rebuild what had been lost. Recil decided to stay behind to lead the way for a new future and rebuild Atlantis and Earth. The Minotaurs and centaurs were the first through the portal; everyone else followed suite. Ky and I were the last ones through the portal.

Everyone was in awe of the beauty of this place. It was very warm and tropical-like. However, it was as though they walked right into a lush green forest with many ferns and odd-looking bushes and wildflowers. Many tall trees. I saw Trish in the distant crowd; she gave me a look as though I had done something wrong. Hearing a waterfall in the distance, Ky and I walked toward the cliff. We got close to the edge of the cliff, holding each other. I was happy. I loved this man very much, and he loved me enough to protect me and comfort me. And I was having his child. This could not get any better.

I looked into his eyes and told him how much I loved him, and we kissed. I looked in the distance towards the waterfall. I could make out a citadel right by it.

"There is it!" I said with excitement.

"There is what?"

"You see that citadel up there?"

"Yes."

"That's where the crystal showed me to go. That is Valendora."

Chapter 23

As Ky and I were walking back to the others, we discussed how Recil decided to stay behind with those who wanted to stay and rebuild Atlantis and Earth. We both felt Recil would be a great leader. I told Ky I wanted to sit and talk first before we met back up with the others. We found a fallen tree that we chose to sit down on.

"I had not discussed with anyone about the crystal. I had completely drained it when I went to it. I have learned so much from that crystal Ky. I know I had spoken in two different languages while in the throne room. From what I had learned from the crystal, I believe it was our previous language before it was lost and the Anunnaki."

"Okay….so what does that have to do with anything? Mother had already gathered information before I met you that we had descended from Mars, and we had made a pact with the Anunnaki to watch over the humans. However, we had no knowledge of after Arcadian had sunk Atlantis."

"Which is what I am getting at. The coordinates the crystal gave me when I was talking in the other language to bring up the portal, it was the Anunnakian language. We are on their planet, in another universe. The Alanteans have not been in contact with the Anunnaki in thousands of years. We do not know how they will react once they find out we are here."

"As you already know, yes, we are decedents from Mars. Our race was called the Tri-Tyrion. Mars was much like Earth at one point in time. Until it was impacted and destroyed, those who were able to flee made their way to Earth for a new beginning. Knowing they would be able to survive. Little did they know of the Anunnaki being there already. They were assisting the humans with their way of life teaching them how to survive. The humans thought of them as their gods. Once we arrived, few humans thought of us as being another type of God. The Anunnaki soon found our race. There was tension between our races. We did not understand them, and thus, they did not understand us. Our languages were different. The Anunnaki were going to attack us, as we were trying to make them understand we were not there to harm them or take over. We just wanted to survive, and a human stepped between the two leaders. The human seemed to understand both of us in a sense. The Anunnaki had backed off and motioned for us to follow them."

"The Anunnaki are different, Ky. They do not look anything like you or me. They are like a lizard. Standing and walking like us, hands similar to ours, but with four fingers with sharp nails, more like claws. Head to body like a bearded dragon. The Anunnaki had built Atlantis and had brought the Tri-Tyrions to it. We lived amongst them, and we learned from each other and to better understand each other. We already had a lot of technology and whatnot, and they had even more. They taught some of us magic and taught some of us how to do gene splicing, and how to build the structures they had. We learned well and continued to build onto Atlantis and build the palace. We also assisted some of the ancient cultures in building theirs that were still standing until the destruction of Earth. They wanted to come back here to their home but wanted to make sure the humans were going to be safe and watched over. To make sure Earth would survive and the humans have peace."

"With the agreement Atlantis would be handed over to the Tri-Tyrion, the two leaders of our races went into the labyrinth, and both placed their hands on the dull crystal that lay before them from the ground to the ceiling; yes, that crystal. Everything from them went into the crystal, all the knowledge and power they held. The crystal is connected to another crystal here on this planet. The connection between the two is very great. If I can find it, I can possibly get more knowledge. More knowledge of this planet and if the Anunnaki are still present. I sense that they are, but I am not sure. The fact that we have not been in touch with them after Atlantis sunk, we do not know how they will take things with us now being here in their world." I explained to him the best I could while trying to understand things that I had not mentioned to him.

"I understand my love. There have been many who have proceeded to leave the area to venture on their own. Hopefully, they will be safe, but there is nothing we can do to stop them. It's a new place, and as much as I would love to keep everyone together, I know we will not be able to. Let's head back to the group before more choose to part ways. We do not know what this world may have in store for us. Maybe you can use your powers when it starts to get dark form some sort of protection around all of us. I know there are many of us, but we can at least try."

"I agree. Let's head back, and we do not know when it will start to get dark. Looks to be a late afternoon, so it may not be that much longer." I did not tell him I felt as though we were being watched.

Ryn watched from a distance on his dragon. Watching many beings coming through some sort of light. They were in flight when he noticed the light appear and these beings coming through. He had Dresden land on the other side of the cliff away from them; as he looked to his right, he could see the old citadel that was abandoned a long time ago near the waterfall. He wondered if they had noticed. He had Dresden make them invisible so he could watch what was happening. He first watched as the Minotaurs came through the portal, along with two centaurs, followed by the humans and the Atlanteans. Wondering what these creatures were, they seemed to be together and getting along. He noticed some carrying items and cages with strange creatures in them.

Reading each other's minds, they are more curious. Is this

the old prophecy coming to light? They decided to keep watch. He was more curious when he saw the last two walking through the light, holding hands. Talking to a few of the others like them, then walking over to the cliff opposite of him. He watched them talk and the female looking over at the waterfall and seeing Valendora.

"Dresden, we should move closer. Land us over there close but not too close. Keep us from being seen."

"I agree; we need to keep watch and see what they are planning. Why are they here, and what do they want? Look at the creatures that are holding the weapons. Look at the metal. That metal you can only find in this realm. How did they get our precious metal to make those things they weld? Are they the ones from the many years past?"

"You are right Dresden. Something is not right. Are they here to destroy us all, or are they of the ancient prophecy?"

As they flew over to the other side, they kept their distance from Jaycenda and her group. Dresden had continued to make himself and Ryn invisible as he flew over to the other side of the cliff. They landed on the cliff Jaycenda, and Ky were at. Trying their best not to make a hard landing and not to make a lot of movement from the wind his wings were producing. They made their way closer, careful not to make much sound; however, with the thumping of the ground with each step Dresden took, he knew they would eventually feel them coming toward them. The forest was thick, and they remained behind plants and trees. Dresden had the better view as he was larger in size and could see from a higher point of view. They watched her as she stood on a large rock, talking to her people. Not understanding anything she was saying in her language, Ryn and Dresden kept watching.

"Everyone, please stay together. We have had many decide to part ways and leave. This is a new world. We do not know what lurks out there. For everyone's safety, we need to stay together. We have the Minotaurs and centaurs here to help protect us. Have you felt the ground? Something is heading our way."

As Jaycenda was speaking, the Minotaurs sensed something and were looking around, grunting and growling, sniffing in the air. They were sensing Dresden and Ryn. They headed towards where they were at. Each wielding their weapons, Bane with the sledgehammer with the spikes, Axel with the Axe, Pike had given his spear a jerk with spikes coming out on the side from the bottom of the speared tip to halfway down the body of the spear, and Makeo wielding two hooked swords and gave both a jerk and sharps blades came out from below the handles. They continued toward Ryn and Dresden, who remained still. The Minotaurs, trying to taunt them forward, kept looking back and forth, still sensing them, but not able to see them; they kept watch. Jaycenda continued to try to keep her people calm and stay together. As it was getting dark, several bonfires were being built. Jaycenda was using her powers to light some of them from the rock she was standing on. This baffled Ryn. How does one have such power?

Jaycenda looked over, seeing the Minotaurs acting up, knowing something was there. Instincts kicked in. She held her hands in front of herself and made an x, then stretched her arms out quickly to her sides and created a protective dome around the group; the Minotaurs started getting fiercer and grunting and growling; the growling was still the most disturbing sound anyone could imagine. They had their weapons ready to go.

"Boys I sense it too. Who or what is there?" as I made my way over, I felt as though whatever was there was not going to harm us. More or less was curious about us.

The dome was right in front of the Minotaurs. I knew something was there, hiding and watching. I concentrated hard as the blue fire began to glow from me. I was trying to communicate with a language from the crystal.

Dresden allowed his slanted yellow eyes to be seen along with the rest of his large black body, revealing himself entirely, and Ryn then appeared. Head shaped like an iguana standing upright like a man. Tail like a crocodile. Unusual Clothing, but it suited him. Scaly skin and was white all over. He had four fingers, much like claws on each hand. He wanted to make contact, and he did by telepathy with Jaycenda, and they were understanding each other in their languages.

Chapter 24

"What are you and what are you doing here?" Ryn asked.

"Our world was pretty much destroyed. I was given coordinates to this place from the crystal that was on our planet called Earth. It gave me a glimpse of Valendora. I am Jaycenda."

Ryn and Dresden looked at each other eyes widened in disbelief.

"I am Ryn. Earth you say? As in the prophecy of the one with the blood of a Tri-Tyrion that beholds the mark?"

"Yes, I think so. What is this prophecy of yours?"

"My people are different from the Anunnaki. We are the Dragonoffs, and we are linked to our dragons. We live a simple life, whereas the Anunnaki are far more advanced and travel to different universes. They leave us alone and stay out of our lands for the most part. We have an agreement with them, but they do not always live up to that agreement. They have changed over the many moons that have passed."

He paused for a moment and looked around as many eyes were laid upon him as he was communicating with Jaycenda with his mind.

"The Anunnaki were once great, and they are still very much powerful. They have traveled to a place called Earth in our ancient past. They had made it a secondary home, and there had been beings that they discovered and were teaching them how to write and build and become more advanced. I believe this would be some of you, I presume. After many years on Earth, they had discovered another race, one that had come from another world. They looked very similar to those that the Anunnaki were teaching; however, they were nearly as advanced as the Anunnaki. These creatures from another world used flying ships, whereas the Anunnaki have traveled through portals. We do not believe they travel anymore and have not for some time. Their leader and the leader of the Anunnaki, Merya, clashed at first but then started to understand each other. The leader had great power and had a mark of two half-moons intertwined. This power they had, it is told that they were able to communicate with the mind, much like you and I."

"The Anunnaki and this race they called themselves the Tri-Tyrion, they started to teach each other some of their ways. The Anunnaki had already been assisting many citadels across many lands on Earth and had provided the knowledge to the Tri-Tyrion. They had described their dwellings much differently. The Tri-Tyrion had described how their homes and markets were made of metals. The Anunnaki had never considered making buildings out of metals. Our world creates the rarest metal called Geolope. It cannot be found anywhere else, not even in another universe. The Anunnaki have created weapons with this metal."

"The Anunnaki is also known for gene splicing. This was another lesson they taught the Tri-Tyrion. Together they had created creatures to protect a crystal with its knowledge and power as it is told, to keep out those who cannot know the entirety of both the Tri-Tyrion and Anunnaki. The Anunnaki used their metals and created the weapons for these creatures, which I believe to be those over there." He stated as he pointed to the Minotaurs.

"They had made five creatures and two charmed necklaces. The Anunnaki mystic who was teaching one of the Tri-Tyrions their magic created the charms; only the chosen were to be able to use the charms to have control over the beasts." His eyes focused on Jaycenda's necklace.

"You are the one!" He said in awe. "That necklace is that described by my ancestors from many moons ago!"

"I do not know what you are speaking of specifically; however yes, this necklace controls the Minotaurs. However, there are only four. The fifth one has been nonexistent, he lives in myths. I also have the mark that you are describing of the intertwined half-moons." I said and then turned and bared my left shoulder, showing the mark.

Ryn and Dresden both took a bow.

"We have waited many, many moons for your arrival. The prophecy was told after the Anunnaki returned. One of our people foresaw Merya would soon be killed upon her return to our world, Dolari. Prior to her death, she and our leader had gone to the great crystal and provided all the knowledge they had about it. This crystal was to be hidden and only few to this day know where it lays. Jorg had overtaken the Anunnaki after Merya's death. He knew of the pact between the Anunnaki and the Tri-Tyrion, as he was by Merya's side throughout they time spent on Earth. Now as many moons passed, contact had remained until no more. No more updates from the Tri-Tyrion After many moons passing."

"The Anunnaki attempted to contact numerous times, to no avail. The leader now of the Annuanki, Leoro, no longer wanted to remain a peaceful civilization. Anyone of my people who dare step into their territory would meet with death. Many times, they tried to find the portal and the coordinates of the Atlantis they left behind. They wanted to take back control. But upon finding nothing, they have thought of it to be a story. They have numerous times wandered into our lands, killing our people or taking them to build on their citadels and or mining the Geolope."

"As the prophecy has been told: A female from another world, another time, who has Tri-Tyrion bloodline and will bear the mark of the intertwined half-moons will appear from light. The day of reckoning after years pass, she will be the arcana of light that saves us all. Bloodshed upon bloodshed until she becomes light. The light that will conquer all. The light that will bring all together."

"I truly believe you are her."

Chapter 25

"Ryn, can you be more specific as to how many years we have? If there is going to be bloodshed, I am assuming this will be a war." I know something big will happen; I can feel it.

"No, the prophetess did not provide that information. Dark days lay ahead. As to how long it is uncertain. You had a vision to bring you here and to Valendora. We had abandoned Valendora not long after the prophet. Possible for your arrival, I do not know. It has gone to ruin. The Anunnaki do not come this far into our lands. I feel you may be safe here. There are secrets that lay within. Drel may know of the location of the crystal. The prophetess and others have given knowledge to the crystal. I feel in time you must go to this crystal. The few that know of its location are Drel and his mate. The Elders only speak with them regarding our secrets of the past. I will go to them and advise them of your arrival. Make your way to Valendora but do so in daylight. It is now dark, and many dangers far worse than daylight lurk in every corner."

"We have had many already leave our group. Will they be safe, or should we assume they have met their fate?"

"I am afraid to say, assume the worst. They are not familiar with our lands, and I cannot say if they would be able to survive. Once I meet with my people, we will assist you to rebuild Valendora and back to its former glory."

"I must go and speak with our elders. Stay in this thing you have surrounding all of you, and you should remain safe.

"Thank you, Ryn. It was a pleasure speaking with you and we will be looking forward to working with your people."

"Yes, it will be of great honor to know and work alongside the one who will bring the light."

Ryn climbed upon Dresden; his wings spread wide. He gave a screech and began to flap his massive wings. They went up vertically until above the trees, then took off as fast as lightning.

As I turned around, all eyes were upon me. I explained that I had been communicating with him with my mind. I reassured them that he and his people would be here to help us. I went into detail about the conversation I had with Ryn. I had advised of the times ahead that will be in store for us, but as far as how long we have until a war is uncertain.

"As soon as daylight breaks, we must make our way to Valendora. Ryn, as he is called, had advised many years ago his people had left Valendora, not knowing when our arrival would be. He stated it was in ruins. I am confident that together, we will restore it to its former glory and make it our own. We will need the farmers that are here with us to begin planting crops and get the chickens a few brought into a safe area. We will have a little bit of home with us at least. Those who are builders, once we get the full layout, we will begin reconstructing the citadel. Those who are unsure of how you can help build our newfound home, we will discover everything together. Ryn will be back to assist us with what we need. In the meantime, let's try to get some rest and begin anew tomorrow." As I stood there, many cheered. I looked in the distance and saw Trish, once again, giving me a look of disgust. I wonder why she has been giving me the looks.

Once the cheers had settled, all of us heard strange noises from afar coming closer until they were right outside of the domed shield, in the bushes and behind the trees several glowing yellow eyes peering at us. They suddenly sprung toward the shield. Gray hairless creatures that walked on all fours. Long rat-like tails, ears like a bat, long snout, and when opening their mouths to bare their teeth and let out unusual growls. Unable to break through the shield, they were getting frustrated. It had gone from several of these creatures to many surrounding the shield.

They were communicating with each other with growls and screeches. One had immediately climbed up a tree and jumped over on top of the dome. Everyone was gasping and frightened. I am afraid they may have gotten to some of those, if not all of those who had left when we had come through the portal. A few more jumped onto the dome. Trying to penetrate the dome with their claws; they became frustrated unable to break through.

The Minotaurs were eager to fight, grunting, wanting to fight. Not knowing if they could handle as many of these things, I advised them to stand down. We all watched with fear and curiosity with these creatures. I know the dome will hold until I release it. I advised everyone we would be safe; the dome was strong, and they could not get through. Everyone is still in fear but tried to rest, but many are unable with the screeches and growls from these things. The centaurs approached, letting me know at the far end of the dome, the creatures had started back away. Where we were, they continued to try to penetrate the dome. Eventually, they had given up and left.

As dawn broke, the centaurs blew their horns for everyone to wake up. I hoped this would not bring the creatures back. We waited for a time to see if they would return; thankfully they did not.

"Everyone, please stay together as we make our way to Valendora. We do not know if those creatures will return. I need two of the Minotaurs in the front and two in the back. The centaurs, please remain in the middle of the group. I know there are many of us, but we will get there." I said as I was standing on the rock again for everyone to hear me. It was a rough night with everyone crowded together. Trying to get rest through the night was not easy, but we somehow managed.

Valendora seemed so close within an hour or so hike, but it

seemed as though it was much longer. Dad and Mom were walking with Ky and I. Dad had pulled out his pocket watch, which did not work on this planet. Mom looked at him and shook her head. I asked her what was wrong.

"Time is much different here, and we will struggle with certain things." Under her breath, she whispered, "There is going to be famine. When this will be, I cannot say. It was a vision I had last night."

"I have not yet had a vision, but I know we will do our best and try to make things work. We may be scarce with food at first, but we will manage. We are already rationing our food supply that some had brought. We will send hunters out later once we reach Valendora and are rested."

"Jaycenda, sweetie, I feel we may reach Valendora by dusk, not before then. Not only that, but there is also either a river or creek that is parting from where we are to Valendora. We will need to find some sort of crossing. Valendora is on the other side of the waterfall."

"This is true. I think we will set forth until we cannot endure any longer. Those creatures have not come back. Maybe they are nocturnal. We need to be on our guard. We have no clue what may lie ahead or even behind us. I don't want another night like last night, but I feel this may be an ongoing occurrence with them. They either considered us as a threat, or they considered us as a new food source. I wish I could communicate with those who have left our group to be on their own."

"I know sweetie. In time, we will discover what has happened, or we may not know. Too many have left.

I looked over at dad. He had remained quiet for most of the time since we arrived. He seemed confused.

"Dad, are you okay?"

"Yeah, I am just dumbfounded by this place. I mean, so far, besides the odd plants, it seems a lot like Earth. But we do not know what is edible here and what is not. The water will it be drinkable for us? There is a lot we need to figure out."

"We will. All of us that are sticking together, we will figure everything out, Dad. Don't worry. Things may be hard at first, but we will survive. Being a leader is something I have never expected; however, I am determined that we will survive. No matter what. I am with child, and I will not let anything happen to us or our people."

"I know sweetie. You have always looked out for everyone's best interests ahead of yours. You have always been that way since you were a little girl."

We managed to go on for hours on end, taking breaks when

needed. As dusk seemed to approach, I went ahead and surrounded us in a dome again. We rationed our food and water once more. As dusk turned into night, we heard the growls and the screeching from afar. Those creatures were back. Once again, climbing up the trees with all fours and jumping on top of the dome in numerous places.

Around the dome, they surrounded us again. Trying to break through the dome once more. After a while, they gave up. I watched one in particular as they started to walk away; the one I kept an eye on looked back, showing its fangs and hissing. When that one hissed at me and started into a run, the others went into a run along with it.

Chapter 26

Dawn broke. Everyone gathered the items they brought with them. Few that had brought chickens rounded up the few eggs that were laid. I managed to get a dozen eggs together and scrambled them. From the many that left on their own, there were fifty of us left sticking together. There was not much to go around; however, we kept rations of our other food sources as well as water that had been brought.

After breakfast and waking up, we once again set foot toward Valendora. We did not have much of a long trek like we had yesterday. We had a hefty trek uphill that took the most toll on us.

On our way, we heard birds chirping and singing to one another. It sounded as though we were in a tropical rainforest, but we were in a lush green forest with a tropical temperature.

We had finally made it to the top of the hill and headed what felt like it was north toward the river. As we approached the river, you could hear the roaring of the waterfall.

The river was fairly large, and Valendora was in sight, not far but not so close to the river. I looked to my left and up the river and noticed a bridge. I urged everyone to head toward the bridge and we will check and see if it is usable.

The bridge was made of stone and arched over the river. It

looked sturdy. Bane volunteered to cross first. He jumped in several areas of the bridge with his entire weight. If Bane was able to cross with no issues, it would be safe for all. And it was.

After everyone crossed, we finally made our way to Valendora. The walls were tall some of the tree limbs reached over the wall into Valendora. As we made our way to the front of the citadel, ivy and roots lingered all over the walls and doors. It took all four Minotaurs to get the doors open. Once inside, we saw the dismay. Most buildings were in ruin, and what looked as though it may have been a palace of sorts was mostly intact; however, areas of it were crumbled. There was a well with a stone over the top and rubble everywhere. We began to enter the village area of the citadel; I knew we would make this place great one day.

The palace was in decent shape. In the village area, people were claiming their homes and those that looked to be once shops; we would decide together as a group what to put in place there. I made sure to let Mom and Dad know they were to be in the palace with us, along with several others and those who sworn their loyalty to serve us in the palace. The Minotaurs never sleep, they would always keep watch. The centaurs would take turns helping everyone in different areas, whether it was using their weight, pulling materials behind them or assisting the Minotaurs with the watch.

That night, we heard the screeches and the growls in the

distance; I knew immediately it was those creatures again. Tracking us, it seemed like. Not knowing that few had been here at the walls. I had created the dome over the citadel, but before it had been created, there had been at least three of those creatures that made it through. As they started to separate and scavenge, the Minotaurs and centaurs started rushing to those who were screaming and running for shelter. One had pounced upon a larger male, clawing his back. He faced down on the ground, crying in agony.

Bane gave his weapon a shake, and the spikes came out. As he went running towards the creature, the creature looked at him, showed its fangs and gave a hissing growl. It had gotten off the male, running on all fours toward Bane. As the creature went into midair like a cat going after its prey, Bane took his weapon and swung it like a bat into the creature. The creature went down on the ground and curled up in a fetal position, twitching and pouting from the impact, and its blood was a dark blue. Bane gave a grunt and then gave his horrid growl, which set fear in the eyes of this creature. He then looked down at the creature, raised his leg and smashed the creature's head with his large foot.

After he gave off his horrid growl, the screeches and growls that were getting closer by the minute had ceased. Whether they had backed away or not, we were uncertain.

The second and third creatures looked at each other when

they saw the Minotaur kill one of their own. The growl from Bane had set fear in them. However, they were not going to give up on trying to get more of our people. As they both started into the running to pounce upon Bane, the other Minotaurs came over to assist.

The centaurs were taking the body of the creature away, and I advised them to store it in a place where no one would be staying, as I wanted to find out from Ryn what these were.

I watched as the Minotaurs were easily taking these things out. Children crying, people screaming with fear. We watched as the Minotaurs were using their weapons and playing with these creatures, having their own fun and games before completely killing them.

That night, I had everyone gather in the palace even though I had the dome over the citadel. Trish still gave me glares. I approached her and asked her what her problem was with me.

She gave a smirk and said, "Well, you know how I once cared for your father? Your mother came back and took that away. I then met Milledge, and things were going great; I told him I loved him even though I didn't. However, it was nice that there was someone who actually did care about me and wanted to spend their life with me by their side."

"Trish, I am sorry about my dad, however he had always

loved my mother. It was love at first sight for them, much like Ky and me. He knew one day she would be back in his life. That is why he never pursued you or anyone. As for Milledge, he wasn't good. Trish, you can and will do so much better. I liked Milledge I had a friendship with him. But it was because of him that Ky thought it was his mother behind everything and killed her to protect me. It was Milledge all along. He wanted to take over."

"It was his right!" she screamed. Mostly, everyone in the room who was awake turned their heads towards us. I grabbed her by the arm and asked to continue this conversation elsewhere.

She moved her arm from my grasp. "We have nothing more to say. If you knew his bloodline was the original royals, you maybe would understand where he was coming from. It was his right through blood."

"Trish, his bloodline wanted complete control over the world. I've seen what the crystal showed me. I know that his bloodline was with one who had the mark of the intertwined half-moons when we first came to Earth. We were known as the Tri-Tyrion. Until another who was born with the mark Arcadian, yes, he had the bloodline. But for those who are born with the mark like myself, whether we want to be a royal or not, it is automatic. I didn't want this, none of this. It was not by choice. If I had a choice, I would have been living a normal life, not having any visions or powers. I have seen a vision of you Trish. You are pregnant.”

Trish gave her an odd look. She had her suspicion but was keeping that to herself.

“Jaycenda, you know nothing. Just stay away from me, and I will do the same.”

“If that is what you wish, I will respect it.” I turned around and walked back over to Ky. Mom and dad were cuddled up, sleeping.

“Jay, my love, what was that all about with Trish?”

“Ky, she blames me for Milledge’s death. And I’m so sorry I have kept this from you. After what happened with your mother. I…. (I started to cry). I’m so sorry to have kept this from you, but you need to know.”

“I need to know what, Jay?”

“After what happened with your mother, I was out fighting those things, and I saw Milledge looking like he was communicating with them. I was right. He was. He said I ruined everything. He was planning on taking over Atlantis. So I had the Minotaurs kill him. Your mother was not behind the war.”

Ky gave me the meanest look I had ever seen. “Jay, I love you, but this… this? You chose to keep from me!”

“Please forgive me, Ky. It wasn’t intentional. I just didn’t know how you would take everything that happened, thinking your mother was behind everything."

"Jay, I love you, but this, this," he said angrily. "I can't look at you right now. He got up and started walking away.

"Ky!" I yelled, "Please come back."

Ky continued to leave the room. I started crying and have never felt so heartbroken and alone.

Mom woke up after hearing me crying. She came over to comfort me and rocked me back and forth until I finally fell asleep.

Chapter 27

The next morning Ky was still avoiding me. This was hurting me deeply. As much as I try to smile, it's the fake smile I would use previously when Logan and I were together.

Many started complaining of not feeling well. The man who was attacked was turning colors and feeling very ill; those who were helping him had become sickened. As I wondered around talking with others, I myself was started to feel sick. I'm not sure if it's the air or what, but everyone seemed to be getting ill. Ky saw me. He looked as though he had a bad case of influenza. He was very sweaty and did not look well. I went over to him and tried to give him some water. He was trying to push me away.

"Ky, I love you, and I am not feeling well either. I promise not to keep anything from you again. You are the love of my life and I do not want to lose you because of my stupidity keeping something from you."

"I know Jay. I love you, and I do not want to be away from you." He said as his shaking hand grabbed the canteen the water was in and took a sip.

He continued, "We have very little food left, and we are all getting sick. Please take care of yourself and our child. If I do not get through this, I want to know that you and our little one will be safe."

"Ky, do not talk like that; we will get through this."

There was a loud banging on the doors to the citadel. It was Ryn with some of his people. Ryn saw me sitting on an old fountain beside Ky. He came over in my direction.

"Ryn, my people and I are not well. We were attacked last night by these creatures. The bodies are over there. One had attacked one of my people who was turning colors. Before turning colors, he was leaking something. Since then everyone seems to have been getting sick. What can we do?"

"Jaycenda, those creatures are called Kurl. They carry poison in their claws. It will make your people sick and possibly kill all of you from the smell of it, just breathing it in from the air."

"Please, Ryn, is there anything you can do to heal my people as well as myself and Ky? I am with child, and I want to bring him or her into this world healthy."

Ryn detached his pouch and had one of his people start a cauldron of boiling water. Ryn discarded the contents into the water and stirred it around. He took a piece of charred bark from the fire underneath and added it to the mixture, stirring it some more. He removed it to let it cool down. He then advised me to drink some of it. Suddenly I felt better. Ky was next, and soon he felt better. Whatever Ryn had done, I was very grateful and indebted to him. I started gathering everyone to come to drink some of the mixture Ryn had made as it was healing those who were sickened. Those who were too weak, I had taken a cup of the mixture to them. It may have tasted completely awful, but it did wonders to make us feel so much better.

Ryn had a few of his people remove the bodies of the Kurl. They said they hunt them for numerous reasons, and since they were recently killed, they were still good for their meals and other uses they had for them.

The man who was injured by them, I discovered his name was Paul. He was human and not one of the Atlanteans. Ryn had gone over and put some type of salve on his injury. Ryn had advised me to let him know not to move around and to have the salve applied three times a day and handed the salve to the woman who had been caring for him.

I explained to the woman what she needed to do for Paul. She thanked me and went back to talking to Paul, letting him know she was there and would continue to help him get better.

Ryn had introduced me to his leader, Drel, his life mate, Ugena, and the Elders who know of the prophecy, Erline and Malise, who were also life mates. They all looked like Ryn, and the females had unusual skirts with matching tops. The Others that were with them were Kane, Regal, and Mylin. Their dragons rested outside the citadel as they were too large to be inside it.

Drel wanted to take me to their city to discuss plans for

Valendora. I advised I would like Ky to come as well as Bray. I advised Bray was an apprentice learning magic.

He agreed. I informed Mom and Dad of what was going on. They agreed to watch over everyone until we returned. The elders of the Dragonoffs went around the citadel walls chanting in their language, and one of them got something from the pouch he carried and sprinkled it around the walls. Ryn had advised that it was to keep the Kurl out of the citadel, and he would have some hunters here tonight on the outskirts to hunt them and to keep them away from us. I was very thankful that this race was friendly and helped us.

Chapter 28

Ky, Bray and I followed Ryn and the others outside the citadel. Ryn advised I could ride with him, Ky with Drel, and Bray with one of the others. As we climbed on the dragons and got situated on the saddle behind the riders, it was amazing to know I was actually going to ride a dragon. Who knew they existed somewhere in time on another planet.

As we went up and were flying it was so amazing. Seeing Valendora from the sky and seeing how massive this world was. The mountains and the forests seemed to go on forever. The air was so fresh, and it was an amazing feeling to know this was where we were supposed to be. No matter the dangers that lurked, we would get through them. As we continued on, we approached a large body of water that looked like it was never ending. It was an ocean, and Ryn pointed to the florescent dolphins jumping in and out of the water. All the dragons started to turn towards the cliffside. There was a large mouth of a cave that we flew into. As the dragons landed, we all got off of them. I was in awe of this place already. The dragons were making their way to the areas where they were kept. Ryn advised that this area of the cave is where the dragons remained and also protected their home.

Drel interrupted and stated that they remained hidden. The Anunnaki were always searching for them even though there was an agreement not to come into their lands, they did not always follow through. He stated they have a killing streak to them now and are not as peaceful as they had once been. He also stated we should not even try to contact them due to the loss of contact many moons ago.

As we made our way through another cave corridor, we had gone down some stairs. Ryn stopped and pointed to his right at an overlook. It was a massive underground citadel, and it was bright. I do not know where they had their lighting come from, but you could see everything. Everything was carved out from the cave and other areas where they had built, which looked a lot like ancient Greece. There were etchings on the cavern walls, a stream running down below, and greenery all over.

We made our way to Drel's home. Even though I was the only one who could communicate, Ky and Bray were in awe of what we were witnessing.

In his sitting chambers, there were wooden benches with soft pillows on them to sit on. They were in a half circle. As we sat on them, Drel and Ryn sat on the other side. His mate went to go back to lay on their eggs, waiting for their children to hatch. He stated they were anxiously waiting for their three little ones to come into this world. He also stated there were three dragon eggs to be hatched at the same time. He said the dragons are their familiars and are linked immediately to them once hatched. The dragons choose their familiar and are raised together.

After discussing how they are linked to their dragons, we began discussing Valendora and how to bring it back to life. He is having builders come the next day to begin helping us and said in the short time, it would be completed. They are also going to be gifting us with animals that we would be able to reproduce to be edible for us, as well as certain vegetables that we would be able to eat. They will help us in any way. He said with me being the one who brings the light, they want this world to be peaceful once again.

I asked him what exactly he meant by the light. I was told only I would know when the timing was right. I asked if he knew anything more about the war ahead. He said he is not certain when it will be, but we all need to be prepared. He wanted us to follow him. We left his home and made our way past the city. We went through another chamber we watched some of his people mining some type of metal. It was the metal Ryn was talking about, the Geolope.

As we made our way passed the mine, we were in a forging area. It was extremely hot from the metal being melted. Some of his people who were working on weapons stopped in awe of us. Two of them took a bow to me. I said hello to them in my mind as I smiled and continued on following Drel and Ryn.

Drel opened a large doorway that led to a massive chamber

filled with different kinds of weapons.

"We have been preparing for the war for a very long time. This is not the only city we have. There are four others like this, and we are all connected through tunnels. The Anunnaki are not aware of our cities now being located underground. Some of us do live above, and that is a risk that they are fully aware of. But together with your powers and what we have, I think we will have a good chance to win this war that is said to come. We believe in our prophecies, as they had always come as told."

"Also, you are not the only ones of your kind here on this planet. The Anunnaki, many moons ago, before losing contact with the Tri-Tyrion, had brought a civilization from Earth. They reside close to the border of us and the Anunnaki territory. We do not bother them. They keep to themselves. They are also the ones who we have been able to get the gifts that will be bestowed upon you."

"Thank you, Drel, and thank you, Ryn, for helping us. I am truly in your debt for everything you have done so far and will be doing to help us here."

"May I see some of your powers? Ryn had mentioned it; however, I would like to see this for myself." He asked.

"Of course, Drel," I said.

I willed the blue fire around me, and I also willed myself to several areas of the chambers. Ryn held up a shield, and I began to cast fireballs at it.

"Impressive!" Drel yelled with excitement. "May I see the mark?"

I turned around and showed him the mark of the intertwined half-moons.

His eyes widened. "Yes! It is true you are the one! We shall train alongside one another until the time has come for us to fight alongside each other. I will have weapons made to suit your kind."

"Thank you Drel. I have been in war, and I know this one will be different, much different. I do feel we will be a great force combined against whatever is to come."

"Yes, we will be. Let's get you all back home now."

Chapter 29

Six months have passed. The Dragonoffs have helped us get the citadel back to what it once was. The gifts they had presented us with were cows and pigs, even horses. It was nice to have some things from home and to be able to gather milk and have meat and horses to ride. The vegetables, some were not like anything we ever had on earth and were tasty. Some things we had brought with us, such as tomatoes and potatoes and corn, grew well here. We were able to eat some of the odd-looking fish that were caught from the river. So far, everything seemed to go well.

We survived two months of a harsh winter. Ryn made us aware these winters would be hard on us, being that we are not used to them. He wasn't kidding. The snow was much colder than on Earth. The temperature went from tropical to below zero for many weeks. Food was becoming scarce, even though we had stocked up prior to the winter; we managed with rationing as we had done so before. We continued to use the calendar that we used on Earth, even though days seemed shorter. This way, we can keep track of everything from the two moons, when to expect the winter and so on. The Dragonoffs thought this was strange as they went by the cycles of the moons.

My stomach was bigger, of course; the little one had done nothing but kick me, and it hurt very much. Ky had been nothing but fantastic, making sure I was always comfortable. I had seen Trish a few times, and she was pregnant as well. She had stopped giving me the strange looks which I was glad she stopped. But out of respect, I stayed away from her.

Nikki and Bray were getting closer. She had opened up to me more over the last few months and understood why I had not said anything about the vision I had about her and Alex. She said she will always love Alex but is trying to move on with Bray and see where things may go. She is thankful to be here but misses her family and Alex. I understood where she was coming from and why she was upset with me. If only I knew when it was going to happen to Alex, maybe I could have prevented it. But I couldn't, and for that, I apologized to her.

Mom and Dad finally got married, and who knew a little baby brother or sister would be on the way? At least my little one would have someone to grow up with. Weird, yes, but who knows what will be in store for all of us. Whether I have a boy or girl, I wanted to name them after Alex. Ky agreed to this.

Ky and I were waiting for our marriage. I did not want to be as big as a whale carrying our child walking down the aisle. We decided after I healed from birth that we would finally marry. I was anxious for our child to come into this world and for us to finally be married. Regardless, if we decide to or not, our love is everlasting.

That night, I went into labor. It was difficult. Ky was holding my hand, and I thought I was going to break it. Mom was there along with someone who we later found out was a doctor. His name was Zach; we did not discover he was a doctor until a few months ago when I had everyone gathered around finding out what type of work they had done previously.

After hours of struggle and pain, she finally made it into this world. We named her Alexis Nicole after Alex and Nikki. Nikki came into the room after everyone had a chance to hold her. I told Zach I was calling him Dr. Z. He laughed and said that would be fine. He left to go check on another patient of his.

Nikki was thankful that we named our daughter after Alex and surprised by Alexis' middle name. She said she hoped to one day become a mother, but for now, she was happy to be an aunt.

Trish heard the news that baby Alexis had arrived. Trish was around the same timeframe. She still wanted revenge on Jaycenda but felt as though she could not do it if she stayed. The next morning, Trish gathered some things in a large satchel and a knife. She decided to leave Valendora but made a promise someday she would be back with a vengeance against Jaycenda.

Trish decided to leave in the early morning. It would be a journey for her. She grabbed a long stick to help her walk. She started walking along the river going North. After what seemed to be several hours, she decided to cross the river by a fallen tree. This area of the river was not as deep and went up to her waist as she crossed. Not knowing what to expect, she wondered will she survive. Will her child survive?

Trish got out a small ration to eat. She noticed a large tree that was hollow at the bottom that she thought she would be able to fit in and rest for the night without any issues. After eating, she gave it a shot, she walked all day and was tired. The night would soon be here, and she did not want to run into any Kurl. She was right. She was able to get in there; it was a tight squeeze with her belly, but she made it. She found a large stone that she put by the entrance; when she made it in, she reached for it, and it covered some of the entrance. She hoped that this would protect her in some way.

As night fell, she heard the growls and screeches from whatever was around, and the loud buzzing of insects. As she was falling asleep, she heard something outside of the tree. Branches crackling, hearing something with heavy breathing and grunting. She remained calm and held her knife ready for whatever may enter.

Whatever it was had left, and she was able to get some sleep. That morning, she pushed the rock over and crawled out from the tree. She ate another small ration, grabbed her walking stick and continued on.

She rubbed her belly and said, "Lil one, we will make it

through this. I promise one day we will have revenge for your father."

By afternoon, she stumbled upon a village made with huts and saw humans. Surprised and happy with this, she decided to make her way to the village. She saw in the background a temple that looked as though it was Mayan. Covered with ivy and mostly hidden, and a farm off to the side of the village.

As she made her way to the village, some stopped what they were doing and looked at her in fright. Trish tried to gesture that she was there in peace as they spoke another language. Similar to Spanish, but it was not Spanish. She attempted a few words in Spanish that she knew of and was looked at curiously.

She placed her hands on her stomach, rubbing her belly. The baby was moving, and she was trying to soothe him or her.

An elder woman pointed toward her, and a crowd gathered behind the elder.

"Obilai! Obilai!" The woman shouted and then moved closer to Trish. She was wearing a necklace with fangs with a gold charm of a lizard head. She had red paint on her face, two streaks of it below her eyes on each side of her face and ashes on her forehead.

She placed her hand on Trish's belly, feeling the baby move.

"Kolachi motolanie crusca!" she yelled for everyone to hear.

Trish was confused; she didn't understand what this woman was saying.

A tribesman brought her over a bowl filled with herbs, and something was making it burn. The woman took the bowl waved the smoke onto Trish, and circled her, doing this and chanting.

Trish had no idea what this was about, but to her, it felt like she was being welcomed.

The woman grabbed Trish's hand and brought her to a hut that was much bigger than the others. From looking around, Trish thought maybe she was the medicine woman.

The woman continued to speak in her language. Trish attempted to speak and received an odd look from the woman. The woman put her finger to her lips, and her eyes got beady. Trish took this as a shut-up and let her do her thing.

The woman gestured for Trish to stand by some smelly furs. As Trish did so, the woman lit a fire, and three other women came into the hut. One with a pot of water that she placed over the fire.

The other two started to strip Trish. Trish is now thinking, what if they are cannibals and she was their dinner? She tried to stop them, and the elder woman shot her a look and yelled something and pointed at her belly. Not knowing what was going on, Trish reluctantly let them finish and they helped her lay down on the furs.

Trish wanted to gag from the smell of them.

Laying there naked, the elder began chanting, and the three other women joined in. It was beautiful, almost heavenly, Trish thought.

The elder took a bowl with the red paint and dipped her thumb in it. She took her thumb and pressed it against Trish's forehead where the "third eye" would be.

They continued chanting. She dipped her finger in the paint again and ran it from the top of Trish's belly to below the belly.

The third woman who came in grabbed Trish by the shoulder, gesturing her to lean up. As Trish did the woman put pillows behind her for support and remained behind her and gestured for her to latch onto her arms as she put her hands on Trish's shoulders. The other two women grabbed her legs and moved them outward. This had Trish thinking something was wrong and fearing for her child.

"Boski! Boski!" the elder woman chanted.

Trish started having severe pain. She began digging her nails into the girl who was grabbing her arms. She wanted to kick her legs but couldn't. She was having excruciating pain beyond belief, and she was crying and screaming and wanting Milledge to be right there.

Trish's vision started to get blurred; she thought she had seen Milledge and smiled through the pain and he was smiling back. She kept looking over at Milledge and could feel their child move more.

The woman was now chanting something different. Trish blinked and continued to look over at the man standing there, smiling at her and realizing it was not Milledge. It was the man who brought the bowl to the elder woman when she first got to the village.

Trish stopped smiling and turned her head back to the elder. One last blood-curdling scream and everything for Trish blackened.

Trish had woken up but was still a bit groggy. She looked toward the doorway into the hut and could see it was nightfall. She was cleaned up and now clothed, much like the other women in the village. She could barely move, and her stomach was smaller. She wondered what happened to her baby. She then heard her baby cry and the elder woman rocking her child back and forth, singing to him in her language.

Trish attempted to talk but was still very weak. The elder had stopped singing and rocking the little one back and forth. She looked over at her and smiled. The baby's cry was now a coo. She came over and brought Trish, her son, wrapped in fur. He was cleaned up and hungry.

Trish unwrapped him to see that the baby was indeed a boy.

Smiling and crying and letting him wrap his hand around her finger, she said, "Hello, my little one. I have been waiting for you. I love you so much. I will name you Milledge Jonathan, after your father and grandfather. MJ for short. What do you think?"

The baby looked up at her, smiling away. She then allowed him to feed. Watching him feed from her breast, she never imagined actually becoming a mother. This was something she always wanted. She wondered why the elder woman had done what she did but was grateful that she had assisted her in bringing MJ into the world. Trish looked over at the woman and said, "thank you." And smiled. Not knowing if the elder understood or not, the elder nodded and smiled.

Trish wondered if she had not found this village, if her son would have made it, let alone herself. She had questions but knew she would not be able to understand them.

A few days passed, and the elder was not around. Trish decided she was going to gather her things and make a harness for her son. As she started to edge the village and head back into the forest, a young child was yelling. As Trish turned around, the child was pointing and yelling "Chimi, Chimi, el-eio!"

Trish turned back around, and standing before her was the same man she saw in the hut that at first she thought was Milledge.

Chapter 30

The man was built much like Milledge and had a shortened beard and mustache. His eyes were very similar to Milledge's.

"El-eio." He said calmly and gestured to the village.

Trish had tried to move past him, he continued to block her way and kept saying "El-eio" and gesturing to the village and smiling. She attempted again, and he said it one last time and chuckled. MJ started to giggle. Trish realized no matter what, she wasn't going to be able to leave and turned back around. MJ had the cutesiest smile she had seen on a baby, and his giggle she couldn't help but smile when he giggled.

For MJ she started back down to the village. The elder woman appeared from another hut. She was talking in her language and pointed to the forest then made an off with the head gesture.

Trish took this as a warning. When Trish spoke, she said she needed to find the Anunnaki. The elder, the man and the child gasped at the name she mentioned.

"Diablos ne Shelu, si." The elder stated while pointing to the golden lizard head charm and grabbing onto the fangs of the necklace she wore.

Trish knew in Spanish diablos was the devil and, of course si for yes. Not knowing what this woman was saying otherwise and it wasn't exactly Spanish she was speaking.

The more Trish pressed in her language, wanting to find the Anunnaki, the angrier the woman got. She gestured for one of the village women to take MJ. Trish was reluctant to give up her child and then realized she really did not have a choice in the matter. She handed MJ over to the woman and began to cry, not knowing if they were going to kill her. What exactly was going on? She wondered.

The elder grabbed her arm and escorted her to the temple. As they made their way through the thick brush and ivy, they made their way inside the temple. The elder had grabbed a torch by the entrance, said a few words and a fire lit up.

They went down a hallway to a large, open room. The elder held the torch up. The room was circular, and back by the far wall was a large statue of a lizard with a human-like body. It was dark and only visible to the light. The statue sat on a large throne holding a scepter.

"Diablos!" The elder pointed to the statue. Then, gesture the off with your head motion again.

The man from the village appeared by them. He gave Trish his torch to hold.

They were talking in their language. He went over to the left of the statue and pushed against it with all of his might. Grunting and catching his breath as it was moving, he continued until a passage appeared.

The elder went in first, grabbing Trish's hand. Trish handed the torch back to the man. The man with shaggy hair, beard and mustache gave her a smile when she handed him the torch; he then followed behind them.

Trish was not in fear of them but more curious about them. She knew they wanted to show her something.

As they descended down a long stairway, they came to a large room with hieroglyphics on the walls.

The elder pointed to what looked to be the beginning of a story.

A planet was shown first that looked much like Earth and a light blue streak connecting from the planet to a portal much like Trish had walked through. In the hieroglyphics, it continued to show what looked like lizard people. Much like Ryn but different. Trish asked if it was the Anunnaki; the elder nodded and continued to show the story, talking in her language, knowing Trish was not able to understand, but maybe understand through the writings. As they continued, it was showing the Anunnaki showing them how to hunt unusual creatures and build a civilization on this planet. It continued on showing timelines and how the Anunnaki no longer would help them and started to take their people for a short time. It then showed a pregnant woman arriving at the village and giving birth to a boy. Trish wondered if this was about her. Did they think she is some sort of prophecy like Ryn thought of Jaycenda? She pondered the thought.

As they continued, it showed the boy growing and learning how to fight and hunt. Becoming a mighty warrior for this village and what also looked similar to Valendora. It also showed the woman being married off to a man in the village who looked similar to the man standing in the room with them. It shows he is the one who will help the child grow and become the warrior he is destined to be.

It then showed there would be a time when a great war would begin. It showed another woman who resembled Jaycenda with some kind of light. Trish frowned upon this, and she wanted to be on the side of the Anunnaki.

As they continued, it showed the young warrior joining forces with the woman with power and a younger woman that looked similar to the woman with power, and the hieroglyphics ended.

Trish was determined that her son would not join forces with Jaycenda. She would raise him to have hatred and disgust for what she did to his father. She wanted Jaycenda dead.

The elder pointed to the married couple. She then pointed to

Trish and the man standing next to her. She then pointed to the birth of the boy raised as a warrior and pointed to Trish, gesturing that it is her son.

They headed back to the village, and it was now nightfall. The villagers were gathered around drums beating, unusual flutes being played, and some of the villagers dancing away.

The villagers started to circle around Trish and the man. Unknowingly to Trish, this was her marriage to this man. A woman blew some sort of powder on them, and another woman started painting Trish's face, and a man was painting on Trish's new husband. One of the villagers adorned Trish with a floral headpiece.

The man took Trish's hand, squeezed it, and looked down at her smiling. Trish then realized this was not an ordinary party they were having, and she was being married off to this man.

The woman caring for MJ brought him over to Trish and her new husband, whom she didn't know his name let alone know his language.

The man took MJ and held him, smiling. He held him up and spoke in his language. The villagers cheered and continued with the music and dancing.

Trish thought this man was ramdsome and kind, but she did not really want anything to do with him but knew she basically had no choice. She knew as long as she remained in the village, she would be safe. She would do what she needed to do to protect her son.

She knew this man would bring MJ up right, teaching him to hunt and become a warrior. She needed to make sure of the importance for MJ to have revenge for his father.

As the ceremony was ending, the man gestured for her to come to his hut. It was a little smaller than the elder woman's. He had a crib made for MJ next to the furs. Trish put MJ in his crib. The man smiled and attempted to communicate with Trish. Neither were understanding one another nor was Trish interested in learning their language.

As years passed MJ was growing up very quickly. He spoke both languages, his mother's and the man who was raising him. MJ always communicated back and forth with them. His mother eventually got to know Ryker's name not long after MJ started talking in complete sentences and understanding both languages. Trish instilled the importance on MJ to have revenge for his real father. She advised him ever since he was little that Ryker was not his real father and that a woman named Jaycenda was responsible for his father's death.

MJ always considered Ryker his father. After all, he was there when he was born; he raised him and loved him as if he were his own son. Eventually, Trish and Ryker did have a child, a boy named Arlo.

MJ and Arlo are five years apart. Arlo was different from MJ. He mainly stayed close to Trish and seldom would he go hunting with MJ and their father. Trish would let Arlo know the importance of MJ's destiny to have revenge on the woman named Jaycenda. Arlo was always confused by this, as she never told him why. He let his mother know he would make sure MJ was aware of what needed to be done.

Chapter 31

Eighteen years had passed. Alexis had grown into a beautiful young woman, looking almost like her mother. She grew up alongside her aunt, who is more like a sister. Emma and Alexis were inseparable. They were never allowed to venture outside of Valendora unless it was with their parents.

Emma had the fiery red hair and crystal blue eyes of their mother. She also had visions, but they were faint, they were not as strong as Jaycenda's or Luciana's.

"Mom, now that I am an adult, I want to venture outside of the walls," Alexis said.

"Alexis dear, no. It is too dangerous out there. I don't want you running into anything out there that may harm you." I told her.

"Your Mother is right, princess. There is too much out there we still do not know about. Yes, you have gone with us to see Ryn and his people. Yes, you have gone on walks with us and fished in the river; yes, I have taught you how to fight and defend yourself. But honey, things are far too dangerous out there." Ky said to his daughter."

"What if Emma comes with me? I want to see some of this world beyond what I know."

"No, sweetie. As your father mentioned, there are things that are far too dangerous that we do not know about." I said, hugging her. "We love you and are only trying to protect you."

Alexis let go of her mother and left the room sobbing. She went to her bedroom. There was a knock on the door.

"Go away!"

"It's Emma."

"Come on in Ems."

"What is going on? I saw you practically running to your room crying."

"Ems, I want adventure. I want to leave Valendora and see what's beyond these walls besides taking trips to see the Dragonoffs and fishing by the river. There is so much more out there to see, and my parents are forbidding me, even though I am now an adult, they forbid me to leave."

"I know you want this. We talked about it all our lives. What if there was a way outside the palace? You know that there are passages all over the palace, and I happen to know of one. I discovered it the other day when you were with your parents visiting Ryn and Drel."

Alexis perked up. "Ems, are you saying you know a way out

without being caught?"

"That is exactly what I am saying, Alexis. I may be your aunt, but you are more like my sister. I will always have your back."

"Will you be coming with me?"

"No, someone has to tell them something to bide your time."

"Well, let's start planning. I want to leave soon. I love you, mom, dad, grams and pap, but I need to do this for myself. This is something I wanted for a long time."

"Give it some time Alexis, do not rush it. You know the stable boy Hans?"

"Yes."

"Well, he has a bit of a crush on me. I can talk him into meeting you at the entrance you will be coming out of with your horse."

"That would be awesome, Ems!"

"And don't worry, I will gather rations for you to take. How long will you be?"

"Honestly, Ems, I don't know. I want to explore, see what is out there."

"Remember what your mom always said about the

Anunnaki, they look different from the Dragonoffs and need to stay far away from them and avoid their territory. Stay within the Dragonoff's lands."

"Yeah, yeah I know. But really, are the Anunnaki that bad?"

"We don't know and do not want to take that chance. There is a reason the Dragonoffs went underground, Alexis. And they have the stories we grew up on about the Anunnaki."

"True, but what if they are different than what we are being told?"

"Alexis, sis, I wouldn't risk that. Remain within the boundaries, please. For me."

"Alright Ems. I won't risk it."

"Thank you." They hugged and discussed the plans further in detail. "We need to see if in the old library there is some sort of map."

"I agree. Let's go look for one."

Emma and Alexis left the room and went to the other side of the palace. They opened the door to the old library that was filled with old scrolls and books. Everything was dusty; they lit candles and were going through all the scrolls that had been left behind from when the Dragonoffs dwelled there.

The scrolls were in writing they did not understand. Emma then came across an old map hidden after going through over a hundred scrolls.

"Alexis look at this!" She brought the map over to a table and laid it out, accidentally ripping some of it.

Alexis came over to see what Emma had found. "Oh wow! Look at this! There was a red line through the center of the map.

"Ok, from looking at this, I am assuming the red line is the boundary of the Anunnaki and the Dragonoffs. But look at this huge citadel over here. That must be the Anunnaki." Alexis said with excitement.

"I think so, we never picked up on the Dragonoff's writings, but I would say stay within the red line. This is where we are right here." Emma said, pointing to the citadel by the waterfall.

"Interesting. I definitely want to learn more of what is over this way." pointing towards an area marked out by the mountains.

"I wonder why it is marked out? There must be a reason. I would stay away from there, Alexis."

"No way! It is an adventure Ems! It is within the boundaries, is it not?"

"It looks like it is. I just want you to be careful. Remember the moves your dad taught you, and you never know if they will come in handy."

"You are right Ems. I'm going to ask for a refresher lesson. Never know if I may need them. I wish I had some of the powers mom has."

"Her powers are pretty cool."

"Alright, let's put this back before anyone notices what we are up to. I have a pretty good idea of where I wanna go explore. I'm excited about this, but I have to keep my cool so no one suspects what is going on."

"Exactly, sis," Emma said as she rolled the scroll back up and put it back in the hidden area where she found it.

The next morning Alexis asked her father to retrain her on some moves to protect herself if she ever needed it. Ky gave her a strange look as she never really cared for the training before, but knowing at some point there would be a war he obliged. They practiced for hours before taking a break. She remembered the moves but was slow in the beginning.

Ky encouraged her to be faster as you never know what the next move will be from your enemy. They continued with the kicks, flips, and using different weapons. Ky reminded her never to underestimate the enemy. Never give a second thought if assumed dead; they may be playing dead, and the next thing you know, you are the one killed. After breaking, they continued on and off throughout the day. Ky wanted to make sure she knew every movement without any hesitation. By the end of the day, she did well, and Ky was very proud of her and gave her a huge hug.

"I am very proud of you, Alexis. You have done extremely well today. It is about time for dinner, and we will pick back up tomorrow."

"Thank you, Father. I want to make sure I know everything you have taught me."

Chapter 32

MJ was ready to become everything he was meant for. He was now eighteen and knew that his time of becoming a warrior was soon. He didn't always care for his mother, constantly telling him he needed to avenge his real father. As far as he was concerned Ryker was his father and called him Father. Ryker loved him as though he was his own.

"Mother I am leaving with Father to go hunting."

Trish gave him a hug. "You stay strong and come back safely. Please do not forget he is not your real father. You need to find a way to seek revenge for his death."

"Mother, that was a long time ago. You have obsessed over this for years! Can you not see the love that father has for you and for me? Can you not see you need to leave the past exactly where it is in the past!"

"Arlo understands, and he knows you need to follow through with this!"

"Arlo has nothing to do with this! You are too obsessed with this Jaycenda person that you cannot seem to let go! Let the past stay in the past! Ryker loves you; he was willing to learn our language, but you were too stubborn to learn theirs. All my life I have been told I am to become a great warrior, well let me be just that! I do not want to hurt anyone! I'm leaving now, Father is waiting for me." MJ walked out of the hut angrily. He was tired of hearing this all the time, and for his little brother to be involved in her scheme made him more upset.

"What is wrong, MJ?" Ryker asked.

"Mother and her you need to get revenge for your real father. I am sick of hearing about it. You are my father, and you have been there since the day I was born. I thank you for that."

"Regardless, you are my son, no matter what," Ryker told him as he placed his hand on his shoulder.

"I had come to love your mother, we were both put into a marriage at the time neither one of us wanted, but it was always up to the elder of the tribe. Your mother had you just a few days before we were married."

"Thank you for coming into our lives. I do not think I would be the man I am today without you, Father."

Ryker smiled. "It was my pleasure to guide you, son, and teach you things you needed to learn. Let's go get some Lanaki to bring home so we can all feast tonight."

Ryker and MJ got on their horses. MJ had the carrier behind

him they would put the carcasses on. It dragged on the ground, but it always suited bringing home the meat.

As they reached their destination in the forest, they tied up the horses. They climbed on the rocks across from one another, sitting high on top. Waiting and listening. Soon, they heard the rumbling coming toward them. The Lanaki. The Lanaki were light tan, with hoofs, four horns, two large above their eyes curling back and two smaller horns that were pointy behind those.

Ryker slowly rose, getting his rope together, making a circle and tying it off. MJ followed suite. As the Lanaki was charging through, Ryker swung his rope and missed. He quickly brought it back up and swung again. This time, he caught one, and they were playing tug of war. This one was not giving up without a fight.

MJ had his bow and arrow ready but could not see which one from the dust, not realizing that Ryker had fallen off the rock and being trampled on. He went ahead and pulled his bow back and took a hit, hoping it was the right one. He then got his rope back up swinging and got one around its neck, it went down and hit hard against the rock he was on. He got excited and looked over, not seeing Ryker, he began to panic.

He hurriedly climbed down the rock, trying to make his way over to the other side where Ryker was. As the Lanaki finished going through, he saw his father lying on the ground, coughing up blood and an arrow through his left side. MJ started to cry and apologized. Ryker was still breathing. MJ carefully place his father on the carrier and quickly untied his horse. He sped as fast as he could back to the village.

Once back at the village, he yelled for help. The elder woman came out and immediately called for others to assist Ryker into her hut.

Hurt and blaming himself MJ went to tell his mother what happened. Tears filled Trish's eyes. Arlo walked in, overhearing what happened, and blamed MJ. MJ knew it was his fault. If he had not gone hunting with him, this would not have happened. Hours went by, and no one knew if Ryker was going to make it. Upset with himself, MJ gathered a few things, got on his horse and left.

Trish yelled for him to come back, but he didn't. He continued on without looking back. He knew not where he was going, but he needed to get away. He did not know how he would deal with more guilt if his father had passed away.

It was close to dawn, and Emma was being sneaky in getting to Alexis' room. She woke Alexis up, letting her know it was time. Hans was going to be waiting for her with her horse. She had a large satchel with bread, fruit and vegetables and a canteen of water in it.

"Emma, I cannot thank you enough for helping me with

this," Alexis whispered.

"Promise me you will come back safe."

"I promise. I just want to go for a day or so. You never know what is out there unless you explore."

"I know Alexis. Just please be safe. If need be, use the moves your dad showed you."

"I will. Let's get going before everyone decides to wake up."

Emma had Alexis follow her to the lowest point of the castle. The dungeon so to speak. It was very eerie, and Alexis remembered why she never came down here. It was cold and damp echoes of water dripping, and it was too creepy for her. It never bothered Emma. She explored this on her own and discovered the passage. They made their way to the end of the dungeon. There was an old torch on the wall. Emma pulled it down, and the wall moved outward. They proceeded through the passage. More echoes of dripping water, and the smell of something utterly disgusting, Alexis wanted to gag. Emma let her know that there is a torch on the other side of the passage that will close the door. They let it remain open until Emma could get back there to move the torch upright to close the door. They made their way to the end and had to crawl out of the tunnel. There Hans was with Alexis' horse.

"Remember Hans do not breathe a word of this to anyone.

Alexis will be back in a day or so." Emma said, giving him a stern look.

"I won't, I promise. I keep my word, and I hope you keep your word, Emma."

Alexis looked at them both. "Um, am I missing something here?"

"Hans smiled and said, "I'm the luckiest guy who will marry the most beautiful redhead in Valendora." He continued to look like a lost puppy in love, looking at Emma.

Alexis gave a gagging motion in which Emma couldn't help but giggle.

"What did I say?" he asked.

Emma looped her arm through his. "Hans, my dear I will keep my word and give you a kiss."

Alexis wondered why Emma was keeping her little romance away from her.

"I better get going before they notice I am gone."

"Safe travels sis. I love you and come back home safe."

"I will. Love you too Ems"

Hans followed Emma into the tunnel that she and Alexis had

come out of. Alexis did not want to think what the two of them were up to.

She started her journey and was heading towards the mountains. Not knowing what was in store for her, she was excited to see what was out there.

Hours went by, and she decided to let her horse, Lilia, rest. They stopped by a creek. She was letting Lilia drink some fresh water.

"Who are you" asked a male voice.

Alexis got up and looked around, not seeing anyone.

Hesitantly, she answered, "I am Alexis. Who are you, and where are you at?"

"My name is MJ," he said as he stepped out from behind a tree.

"What are you doing out here by yourself? There are dangers that lurk around, you know."

"So, are you saying you are dangerous?" Alexis said with a giggle. She found him to be very attractive and liked his short black curly hair.

"Well, no not me. I have never seen you before, and these forests will not be kind to you."

"Well, MJ, who says I am alone?"

"The fact that I saw you riding up here by yourself and no one else around."

"Oh, so you were spying on me?"

"No, I notice things."

"So, if it's so dangerous, MJ, then why are you out here alone?"

"I am a hunter and a warrior, and I know how to take care of myself."

"Then MJ, how do you know I do not know how to take care of myself?"

"Well, because you are a girl."

"Technically, a woman I just turned eighteen a few days ago."

"Interesting because I also just recently turned eighteen."

"So, what does MJ stand for, or is that really your name?"

"It is short for Milledge Jonathan."

The name Milledge rang a bell but Alexis could not remember where she had heard of that name before, as it was a very long time ago.

MJ started making his way over to Alexis. She was blushing but decided to get up. As he approached her, she was standing her guard with a knife in her left hand.

He laughed. "Really?"

"Yes," she said, being very serious.

I'm not going to hurt you. I do not believe in hurting a woman.

"Is that so?"

"Yes, it is so Alexis."

"How do I know I can trust you?"

He circled around her. "You don't, but I can assure you, eventually, you can learn to trust me. I must say you are the most beautiful woman I have ever seen."

"Is that so, MJ?"

"It is." He said with a smile and a wink.

Her heart was beating fast, and she was feeling weak in her knees. She was shaking like a leaf, not because she was nervous, but because she wanted to know him more.

"Well MJ, you are not so bad looking yourself."

"Meaning?"

"Meaning I do find you attractive."

"May I have your permission?"

"Permission for what?"

"May I have your permission?"

She giggled and said sure.

MJ gave her a very nice, long, passionate kiss and stepped back away from her, holding her hand.

"Wow, I must say that kiss was amazing," Alexis said.

He winked at her.

"Thank you." He said smiling. "So, what is someone like you doing out here, and where are you from?"

"I wanted an adventure, and so here I am. As far as where I am from, does that really matter?"

"Well, I suppose it doesn't, but I am curious as I have never seen you before. As for adventure, I could use some. Care if I join you? You may just need a protector."

Alexis smiled bond blushed. "Well, I suppose I could tell you, however, in due time. We always managed to keep our place secretive. And if you truly wish to join me, you may."

"Fair enough, when you decide to tell me, then I will tell you where I am from."

"Fine." She said, looking at him and wanting him to kiss her again.

"Fine." He said smiling at her.

He whistled with his fingers, and his horse came running over.

"That is neat. I cannot do that."

"It takes practice. So where are we off to?"

"Um…." Alexis looked around, trying to find the peak of the mountain she had seen on the map.

"I think I need to go further to see. But I know I have to remain in the boundaries of these lands."

"Boundaries? There is a whole world out there."

"Yes, but have you heard of the Anunnaki?"

"I have. My village calls them the Diablos."

"So you know they are not exactly friendly, right?"

"But who says we are gonna get caught?"

"True. But there is something on a map I saw that I wanted to check out, only I don't remember which way to go."

"Well then, let's be off, and if anything comes to mind, you just let me know, and we will start making our way there."

"That sounds great, MJ."

Chapter 33

It had been a few days that passed. MJ and Alexis had gotten to know one another. He had shown her how to use his bow and arrow. They wrestled around, showing off the moves they had to one another.

They made a camp by a nearby creek that had a deep area. Alexis made her way down to take a bath. She forgot her soap and turned around to get it from the saddle on Lilia.

"What are you doing?"

"I'm going down to the creek to bathe. Don't be watching now." Alexis said with a smile at MJ.

"Well, I'm next." He laughed.

MJ couldn't help but watch. He would hurriedly look in the opposite direction if, for a moment, he thought she would be looking back at him.

"Come join me, MJ; I'm about finished."

MJ hurriedly made his way down to the creek and got undressed. Alexis kept her back turned out of respect and the fact she had never seen a naked man before.

As she handed him the soap, he grabbed her and kissed her.

She reciprocated for a while. She stopped when he got closer, and she felt him. She immediately let go and got out of the creek, grabbed her clothes and went up by the horses.

"Is something wrong, Alexis?" He asked upset by the way she had left.

"Um, nope, just needed to check on Lilia here and figured I'd check on your horse as well."

MJ hurried up, finished bathing and made his way back to the camp. He grabbed his bow and arrows and went to go hunting. Alexis thought he was mad at her and started to cry.

An hour later, he was back with a large bird. Alexis was happy to see him back. He showed her how to pluck the feathers off and prepare it for cooking. She was disgusted by it, but she has seen worse, such as MJ cutting off its head.

Alexis had a small pouch of herbs that she had sprinkled all over the bird after washing it off. They roasted the bird over the fire.

During dinner, they talked. MJ let her know after knowing her for a few days he wanted to claim her. She asked what he meant by that he said he wanted her to be his life mate.

Alexis couldn't stop smiling, and she agreed to be his.

That night, under the stars and blankets, they made love.

Neither expected this to happen or for feelings to get involved, but they decided they were going to be together regardless of anything that stood in their way.

Afterwards, he was holding her. They were both tired but kept small talk going. She finally let him know she was from Valendora.

He said he had heard of it, and his mother had once been there before leaving. He asked her if she knew anyone by the name of Jaycenda.

"Yes, that is my mother."

"Are you serious?"

"Yes, why? What do you know of her?"

"My mother knows of her. Trish. I was named after my father, Milledge. She always blamed Jaycenda for his death but never went into detail."

Alexis then recalled where she had heard the name Milledge before: "My Mother is a good person, MJ. We are originally not from this planet. Mom had told me the stories of Earth and when Atlantis rose from the ocean. She told of the story of Milledge, whom she thought was a friend, but in turn, the one who had created and released these creatures that were killing everyone in sight.

Mother had no choice but to kill him, he was linked to the creatures he created."

"So, my father wasn't this great man my mother would make him out to be."

"I am sorry, MJ, that is the story. My mother doesn't lie, and those who were there say the same."

"Thank you for telling me the story and not keeping it from me Alexis."

"Anything for you, MJ." Alexis rolled over, feeling guilty for telling him, but if he never knew, he had a right to know. She felt more comfortable when he rolled over and was holding her.

The next morning, they cleaned up the campsite. He asked her if she wanted to stop off at his village. He wanted to check on the status of his father, who raised him and his mother and brother Arlo.

She agreed. As they made their way to the village she was getting stared at, it made her feel uncomfortable. MJ smiled at her and grabbed her hand. He greeted the villagers and held their hands up, letting them know he now had a life mate. The villagers cheered and started to prep for their ceremony that night.

Alexis asked what that was about, and he advised her they

would marry them off that night. He went to check on his father, thankful he made it. Ryker was thankful to see his son and looked over to Alexis and smiled. He pointed and asked MJ how he met her, and he explained.

"Where is Mother and Arlo?"

"They will be back shortly, and they went to gather some vegetables for tonight's stew."

"Well, the village is starting to prep for our ceremony. Alexis had agreed to be my life mate.

"Son, that is wonderful, and I am so happy for you!"

Arlo came into the hut, continuing a conversation with Trish. As soon as Trish came in and saw Alexis, when she turned around, she dropped her basket letting all the vegetables fall out and roll all over.

"What the hell are you doing here, Jaycenda? Stay away from my family." She started to lunge at Alexis, pulling her hair and trying to choke her. Ryker and MJ got Trish off of Alexis. Arlo just stared, waiting to see what would happen next.

"Mom, this is not Jaycenda this is Alexis!"

Alexis had tears in her eyes and was rubbing the area her hair was being pulled at.

"Oh, her daughter. Sorry, Alexis, but your mother has it coming!" She said in a hateful voice.

"Mother stop! She is going to be my life mate!"

"The hell she is! You better find someone else or I will. She will never be part of this family!"

Ryker intervened, "Trish I grew to love you, but all these years you had such hatred for someone because of something that happened to MJ's real father. It is time to let it go."

"NEVER!" She yelled and stomped out of the hut.

"MJ I am truly sorry for how your mother is with all of this."

"It's ok Father. As long as Alexis is by my side everything is the way it should be." Ryker gave them both a big hug.

That night, the drums and flutes were being played away. They had the powder blown on them and their faces painted. Alexis was adorned with a floral headpiece placed on her head. Afterwards, they all had a feast. Trish wanted no part of the ceremony. She felt her son betrayed her. She gathered some things in a satchel and decided to go find the Anunnaki. She would make Jaycenda pay one way or another, and now that her daughter got in the way of her family, why not have her taken out, too?

After the ceremony they went to a hut that had been given to them and spent the remainder of the night. They discussed in the morning they would leave the village to continue on their adventure. Neither Alexis nor MJ could believe they were married. Alexis informed MJ how different the ceremonies are and he was interested in seeing how they did them in Valendora.

Ryker knew what Trish was up to. He started to track her into the forest. He had finally caught up with her.

"Trish, stop this nonsense! Come back to the village now!"

"Ryker, I care for you. But you have no idea what I have been through. That girl is no good for MJ! She's part of Jaycenda, and if I have to have her offed too to keep her away from MJ, I will!"

"Trish, I grew to love you, but this is beyond insane! Let the past go! It cannot be changed!"

"You are correct. It cannot be changed, but I can have the person responsible taken out!"

"Get back to the village now, Trish." He said very angrily and pointed the way back.

"No!"

Ryker picked her up and carried her over his shoulder. He quickly started walking back to the village.

The evil look in Trish's eyes she was determined to do what

she was planning to do.

She reached back on her belt where her knife was in its holder. She carefully and slowly pulled it out. As soon as she was able to wield the knife with both hands, she stabbed Ryker directly in his back.

He dropped her on the ground as he fell and looked up at her, asking why she couldn't let go and that she was loved. He then collapsed.

Trish looked at him and, got an evil smirk, and continued on her way. She wasn't feeling guilty for what she had done. He was getting in her way of what needed to be done.

As dawn broke, Alexis and MJ gathered up their things to continue their adventure. MJ wanted to say goodbye to his family. Arlo told MJ neither their mother nor father was there. He had just woken up and did not know how long they were gone.

"Please let them know we came to say our goodbyes for now. We are going to continue on our little adventure that we began with." He said, looking happily in love with Alexis.

"I will. Be safe." Arlo told them and gave his brother a hug. He gave Alexis an odd look.

They continued their way past the temple opposite where

Ryker lay. After hours of traveling, they rested. Alexis noticed an odd-looking skull on a spike.

"I think we are at one of the border points, MJ. I would assume this skull means to stay out."

"I believe you are right. Let's go take a peek though, shall we?"

As they climbed up the small hill they were still in the forest. Looking down was a steep hill, then a large open range with a river running through it. They saw in the distance a large city mostly surrounded by mountains.

"I do not think this is a good idea, MJ. We should head back."

"No! Wait! I have not seen anything like this before!" Looking to his left, he saw two Anunnaki making their way in a hurry towards the city. They were on a hovering craft and had a cage loaded on it.

As MJ looked closer, it was his mother in the cage.

Panic set in.

"MJ what is it?"

"They have my mother! I do not see my father. I have to go after her!"

"MJ, we must not cross the border further!"

"That is my mother! If it was your mother, you would want to go and save her as well!"

"You are right, but we cannot go in there foolishly, MJ! We need to figure out a plan."

Not knowing what was lurking below them, An Anunnaki rose before them, wearing a jet pack. He started talking to them, but neither understood. He raised his weapon, pointing it toward both of them.

MJ stepped forward, and another rose up and grabbed him, taking him to a cage down below. Alexis, in fear, stepped back and fell backwards, rolling down the hill they had gone up. Laying their unconscious, the Anunnaki came over the border to see her lying there and not moving. He proceeded back.

Hours went by. Alexis was coming around.

"Oh my head hurts. What is happening?" She said as she was slowly opening her eyes and getting herself up. She was hurting all over.

"MJ? MJ? Where are you?" It was dark, but with the light of the moons, she could see where she was at.

The horses were still there. MJ was nowhere to be found.

She then remembered what happened. She ran back up the hill she saw the large city in the distance all lit up. She ran back down the hill. She hurriedly got on Lilia and grabbed the reigns of MJ's horse. She made her way back to the village and found Arlo. She explained to him what happened and asked him to inform the village. She was going to make her way back to her home to get her people to help.

As Alexis was making her way back home, the Kurl started to chase her. She was in an open field and praying she would make it through the night as long as they kept their distance. As they proceeded to get closer, a large roar from the sky came and set the Kurl ablaze. It was Dresden, he and Ryn had found her. One Kurl was off to the side and lunged at Lilia. Lilia went down squealing in pain, throwing Alexis off.

Dresden landed, and Ryn took care the Kurl that took Lilia down.

"Thank you, Ryn."

He nodded and helped her get on Dresden they rode back to Valendora.

As Alexis entered the palace, Jaycenda and Ky gave her the biggest, longest hug. Followed by Luciana, Sam and Emma.

"Where were you? We have been so worried about you! If it were not for my vision of Ryn rescuing you, I do not know what would have happened!" I said, upset and happy she was home at the same time.

"I wanted to explore the lands. I met someone, MJ. He and I had been married in his village. The only problem is his mother is your enemy, Trish. While we were off exploring, we went by the border he saw his mom in a cage being led towards a large city practically surrounded by mountains. Then, somehow, they caught MJ, and I slipped and fell. They left me but took him. Mom, we have to save him, he is my husband."

I had a vision. They were coming. They were coming to Valendora because of Trish. And they were on their way now.

"Ring the bells. Have everyone go underground into the tunnels now!" I yelled.

As the bells rang, everyone started to scramble and some screaming. This was not a test; this was the real thing coming.

I communicated with Ryn, thanking him for saving my daughter. I advised him the time had come, and the Anunnaki, regardless, were on their way.

Ryn took off on Dresden and went to inform Drel and the other Dragonoffs that the time had come. Ryn let her know they will help them in any way.

Everyone came to the palace and went down a passageway to an underground area that she had the Dragonoffs help create. Here they had plenty of food and water to last all of them for several weeks. Jaycenda sealed off the wall until she knew it would be safe for them to return above.

The Minotaurs and centaurs wanted to stay and above and protect everyone and the city. Jaycenda knew the Minotaurs would be fine but was not sure about the centaurs. She tried talking them into staying with everyone in the hidden chambers, but they refused. They wanted to try to protect what they could.

Chapter 34

Trish tried her best to communicate with the Anunnaki. She wanted so badly for them to go after Jaycenda. She then saw another bringing in a cage and placed it next to hers. She immediately realized they had captured MJ.

"MJ?" She cried out.

"Mother, what are you doing here? Where is Father?"

"Ryker is dead, and I am going to strike a deal for us to get us out of here."

MJ sat back, shocked, and started to cry. He couldn't believe his father was gone for good this time. He wanted every Anunnaki to pay for this. He certainly did not like how he was now witnessing how his mother was being treated. This angered him even more. He was giving one of the guards the look of death, and the guard seemed to laugh it off.

One of the Anunnaki came and unlocked her cage, grabbing her by her hair and forcing her out of it, letting go of her hair and causing her to fall. He then gestured for her to go forward. She got up and started walking forward. Trish kept being pushed whenever she would slow down. The Anunnaki brought her to their leader. He looked much like the statue in the temple, sitting on a throne holding a scepter.

Trish tried to explain of coming through a portal from Atlantis and she knew where Jaycenda was, the High Queen. She also was trying to explain the powers Jaycenda had.

Neither Anunnaki understood what she was saying. She tried to draw out the story with her finger on the floor.

The leader rose up and began speaking in his language. He pounded the bottom of the scepter on the floor. A hologram of their planet appeared.

She tried to describe with her hands another planet. They looked at her oddly, and some laughed at her.

He pounded the scepter again, and a hologram appeared. It was of Earth.

Trish gave a smile and a thumbs up. She pointed to where she thought Atlantis was and then made a motion that they came from here. She was trying to let them know she came through a portal.

There was talk amongst the Anunnaki.

She walked around the first hologram and saw the waterfall by Valendora, only there was no Valendora on the hologram. She pointed to it and looked up at them.

"Here, right here, is where you will find that bitch!" she said, proud that she was able to point them where they needed to be.

They looked at her like she was going to be their dinner. She was frightened but satisfied with letting them know where Jaycenda was. Even if they were to kill her, they knew where Valendora was located.

The leader started to speak to all in the room. He wanted to gather some of his warriors and go further into the Dragonoff's lands. He wanted to see if this human before them was truthful about something being by the waterfall.

As the warriors gathered outside of the city with their hovering crafts, Trish was placed in the first one, sitting between the two of them. She tried to get comfortable, and she felt like she was going to be crushed between them.

They made their way to the waterfall and saw Valendora. They hovered down into the citadel. At least fifteen warriors looked around, not finding anyone in sight. They saw where fires had recently been extinguished. They noticed the farm and animals.

Knowing somehow whoever was here was informed of their coming. They started to destroy Valendora. Two of them went to the outskirts and lit the farm on fire. They started to destroy the buildings. Ryn came in strong with Dresden with the invisibility; alongside them remaining invisible were Drel, Ugena, Erline,

Malise, Mylin, and Kane on their dragons. They saw Valendora being destroyed as they were riding in. As two of the Anunnaki got on their crafts, they were ascending above Valendora; Dresen made himself known in front of one. Larger than the craft, he opened his mouth and, set the craft ablaze and went crashing down into one of the buildings. Each craft that was grounded was taken out so they could not escape. Only one craft made it out, and that was the one Trish was in.

The Minotaurs were anxious to play. As the Anunnaki were not concerned with the crafts being destroyed, they were more concerned with finding anything alive and destroying Valendora.

Bane made himself known and gave his loud roar and pounded his chest. Two Anunnaki looked at him oddly and wondered what exactly he was. One pointed his weapon at him and took a shot at him. Not fazing Bane, he looked at his arm where it grazed him and saw his burnt hair. Bane raised his head and gave out the most god-awful roar he had ever given, along with the look of death to the Anunnaki that shot him. He went running towards both Anunnaki, shook his weapon, smashed his sledgehammer into the one that shot him, then ran over, placed his foot on its chest, took his weapon, and brought it down on its head, smashing it. He looked over at the other Anunnaki, and it took off running. Bane went chasing after him.

Another Anunnaki was being chased by Makeo and Pike. It decided to scale up a wall. Pike threw his spear into its back, and it fell backwards and further on the spear once it hit the ground. Another was looking at Makeo and shape-shifted into him. Makeo and Pike looked at each other, confused. Axel saw the Anunnaki transform into Makeo and came up behind it and chopped its head off. Other Anunnaki that was watching and seeing what was going on decided to flee. Both centaurs went chasing after them and got caught in the crossfire between the Anunnaki and the Dragonoffs.

Trying to get behind the Dragonoffs, Drel's dragon could not maintain control and burnt both the centaurs and the Anunnaki.

The surviving Anunnaki and Trish made their way back to the citadel. One kept their weapon on her. She knew one sudden move and they would take her out. They felt betrayed by her. She led them there and they were the only ones to return.

They forced her to the ground in front of the leader. In their language they told him of what happened and how the Dragonoffs arrived with their dragons.

He had one of the guards take her off to a cell. A few doors down from her son.

"MJ? MJ, can you hear me?"

"Yes, Mother, are you alright?"

"Yes. I showed them Valendora. We went, but no one was around. They were destroying it until those Dragonoffs arrived."

"You did what? For your stupid revenge? I don't care about it. I want my wife and I don't know what happened to her."

"It is not stupid! You never had the chance to know your real father! As for that, Alexis, you can do so much better, MJ!"

"She is what I want. We are done Mother. Nothing can get through to you. Common sense left you a very long time ago."

They remained silent. MJ was thinking of a way to escape. He decided if he could he would not risk trying to save his Mother. He loved her dearly but was tired of everything that she wanted.

MJ grabbed onto the bars on the window looking out at the stars. Soon it would be dawn. How much longer will the Anunnaki keep them alive? He desperately wanted to get back to Alexis. He noticed one of the bars was loose. He continued to move it back and forth. He finally got it free, and he tried to work on another. It wasn't until he noticed the stone above that was holding the bars in place was crumbling. He took the bar he removed and kept chipping away at it. His Mother asked what he was doing he told her it was nothing, just go back to sleep.

After a while, MJ was able to squeeze through. It was a tight squeeze, but he made it. The river down below was his only means to escape. He jumped into the river; he came up gasping for air as the current caught him, trying to pull him under.

It carried him away outside of the city and into the middle of the range. As he reached the shore, he lay there, thankful he made it through that. He was more thankful when he saw several lanaki grazing. He gathered his strength and started running towards them. He was able to grab ahold of one and climb upon it. He grabbed onto its front horns. It was trying to buck him off and then went running into the forest. It crossed the border, and he was back in safe lands again.

The lanaki continued to try to get MJ off of it and rammed its head into a tree, trying to smash his hands that were holding on to its front horns. MJ got the hint and got off. He realized where he was at. He started running for the next thirty minutes and came upon his village. He hurried to his home. He quickly changed clothes.

Arlo asked what was going on, he told him that Alexis came by and told him what happened and left for Valendora. MJ explained to him what had happened and that he had to get to Alexis. He wasn't sure of the way, but he wanted to make sure she was safe. Arlo refused to go along with him; he said it wouldn't be fair to Mother to knowing her feelings toward Jaycenda. MJ gave him a scornful look and left without a goodbye.

Chapter 35

Everyone was trying to remain calm as they could hear the rumbling and feel the buildings being destroyed above. Jaycenda wanted desperately to go and use her powers against whatever was there but did not want to risk the lives of her family or people.

She had everyone stay below for another day before going above to see what happened. All of their live stalk, their vegetables and other crops gone. Thankfully, they had enough food stored away to last for a little while. They would need to ration them. Ryn and some other Dragonoffs were trying to rebuild the city again for them.

"Ryn, you know the Anunnaki more than any of us. How much time can we have before they all-out war?"

"Jaycenda I can tell you within what you would call a few days' time. We need to get you to the crystal. It is time."

Drel and Ugena were arguing over the location where the crystal was located. Jaycenda felt it was no use, and they were not really sure. She advised her family that they may never find the crystal. Emma recalled the map she found with a marked out area. She remembered putting it back in the hidden compartment she found it in after she and Alexis had looked at it. She ran off to get it.

Emma came back with the map and laid it out. She pointed to the area that had been marked out. Drel looked at it and pointed and said something to Ugena in their language and laughed.

Jaycenda interrupted them. "I know we don't have much time. Drel, can you take me there?"

"Yes, of course. I recommend Ryn and Ky come along. I have heard stories of our ancestral burial tomb but have never gone. There were warnings in place to keep others out. Especially those who are not Dragonoff. As to why this was marked off the map, I can only wonder if that is where the crystal may lay." He told her.

"I feel that it is."

"Then we must make haste."

Drel assisted me in getting onto his dragon. Ky rode with Ryn. We flew over mountains and valleys that we had never flown over before with them. The beauty of this world, and we haven't even seen half of it.

We had approached the largest mountains I have ever seen, including on Earth. The dragons landed at the bottom near a cave entrance. We dismounted the dragons and walked closer to the entrance.

Drel and Ryn picked up two torches, and I lit them with my

power. Drel went in first. Ryn gestured for Ky and me to follow Drel. It was more of a tunneled pathway. Water was dripping and echoing, but from where was unknown. As we continued walking, we saw a light at the other end of the tunnel.

As we stepped out of the cave, we were underneath a waterfall that ran off into a stream. As we stepped aside from under the waterfall, we were all in awe of the beauty of the gorge. Drel and Ryn extinguished their torches and took the lead, walking up the stream.

The gorge is surrounded by mountains, luscious ferns, moss, and plants that we have not seen anywhere else on this planet. In the distance, you could hear more waterfalls. Two large carvings of Dragonoff ancestors holding their weapons were facing each other with the stream running between them.

The detail was amazing, as though they had been perfectly preserved. We continued to walk through the narrow stream toward the statues. As we passed the statues, you could hear the fierce roaring of the waterfalls. Coming around the bend, there were three waterfalls, one in the middle, one on the left the other on the right. Between the waterfalls were carved heads of dragons. We noticed the waterfalls were descending into the blackened cave below. I looked over the edge into complete blackness.

Drel found a pathway off to our right that went behind the

first waterfall. Behind the waterfall was another cave entrance with an inscription above it and small dragons carved on each side facing the entranceway.

Drel stated that it was the warning he had mentioned previously. He mentioned he did not believe there was anything that would do us any harm, as he felt it was more to scare others who may enter that were not of Dragonoff Clan. He strongly believed this was where the crystal was hidden.

I could feel its presence. I was immediately drawn to it. I willed the blue flame as Drel, and I entered. Ryn and Ky remained behind. Ky felt it would not be right for him to enter and expressed this in signing to Ryn and Drel. I told him I understood and blew him a kiss. He acted like he caught it and gave me a wink and a smile.

I relit Drel's torch. He took the lead as we went down the carved stairway. As we came to the bottom, I could hear the waterfalls crashing into the river below. We crossed an old wooden bridge that we thought for sure was going to break on us. We came to the other side, and there were two large doors. The presence of the crystal was growing.

We tried pushing the doors open, but there were no handles. The doors did not want to budge; I pushed my arms outward, letting my power flow through me, and pushed the doors open.

Upon entering the chamber, there were more lifelike carvings of dragons and four Dragonoffs, with only one difference: these statues had wings.

"Drel, why do these carvings have wings?"

"It is said that many, many moons ago, when we had come into existence, we were able to fly and fight alongside our dragons. As many moons came to pass it is said that our leader had lost a great battle and was shamed. It is said that our creator had taken our wings as a sacrifice for our loss. This is prior to the Anunnaki. The battle was with others from another world. They had come to take whatever they wanted from our realm. They had killed some of the greatest warriors and their dragons. After the battle, those beings had never been seen since. I believe these carvings are in their honor. As you know we continue to fight along with our dragons, just differently. It would be interesting to know what it is like to fly side by side with my familiar. However, it will never be possible."

"I think I understand."

"Come, Jaycenda, let's continue on our way, and I see a passage over this way."

"Yes, Drel, I can feel the crystal. It keeps getting stronger. I just cannot pinpoint its exact….." I stopped talking as it grew even stronger. The blue fire around me suddenly grew more. I was drawn to walk past the statues to the far end of the chamber.

Drel looked at me in disbelief and asked how I was flying toward the wall. I told him I wasn't, that I was walking. As I looked down, he was correct I was floating toward the wall.

Drel came rushing over by me when I landed infront of the wall. It was just part of the mountain, and I did not understand.

It then dawned on me. "Drel, this is not a tomb of your ancestors."

"What do you mean, Jaycenda? We must go down the path. There is nothing here but stone. We need to get to the tombs."

"You don't see the inscription?"

"What inscription?"

As he asked about the inscription, I started chanting in a long-forgotten language. Drel was in amazement as he continued to watch me. As I was chanting each part of the inscription it would light up in gold before disappearing.

When the inscription would light up and disappear that is when Drel was able to witness the inscription Jaycenda was talking about. He was shocked and speechless.

He could briefly make out the inscription as it was disappearing as quickly as she chanted. All he could make out was the Arcana of Light.

When I finished chanting, we could feel the shaking of the ground and the rumbling of the wall moving backwards. It was just enough space for us to walk through into another chamber.

The blue flame around me ended as I entered the chamber. In the middle of the chamber, standing vertically, was the crystal glowing brightly; it hovered above a circle with additional writings around it and unusual patterns within it glowing purple. Drel attempted to get close to it. I put my arm in front of him and shook my head. I knew if he had entered the circle, He would meet his end. It was an enchantment put in place. Only the Arcana of light can go into the circle.

As I had explained this to Drel he then understood and backed away. He watched as I entered the circle. I looked up at the large crystal. As I placed my hands on it, a gust of wind came, blowing my hair back. I could feel all of the energy and additional power. One like I have never felt before. After I had gathered what I needed from the crystal, it fell to the ground, landing horizontally. The glowing circle remained.

I stepped out of the circle, feeling dizzy and weak. As I started talking to Drel, everything became dark. I could hear him trying to wake me to no avail. I felt him pick me up, place me over his shoulder, and carry me out.

Ky was keeping an eye out on the entrance as it had been some time since Jaycenda and Drel had entered the cave. They arrived in the morning, and it was now afternoon. He then saw Drel emerge from the cave carrying Jaycenda over his shoulder and a torch in his left hand. Ky ran over to help assist in getting Jaycenda down as Ryn was taking the torch off of him.

"Jay sweetie." He said as he was trying to wake me up. "I know you are weak, and we must get you back to Valendora and rest."

I slowly opened my eyes and saw Ky's face. I told him I loved him and Alexis before I closed my eyes again.

Ky carried Jaycenda as they quickly made their way through the gorge and tunnel. They got on the dragons and flew off to Valendora.

Once they arrived. Ky, Luciana, and Sam made sure Jaycenda was resting comfortably. Alexis was talking to Emma about how worried she was about her mother and not knowing what happened to MJ. She then stopped as she was having her first vision.

Chapter 36

One of the Anunnaki guards brought Trish to one of the mystics. As Trish looked directly into the mystic's eyes, she saw it shapeshift into her. Shocked that this thing had now looked exactly like her, she yelled out, "What the hell?"

As she did so, the guard came up behind her. He grabbed her head and twisted it, throwing her body onto the floor.

The Anunnaki were preparing for war. The mystic looked at the guard and gave him a smirk as she grabbed his knife. She got onto a horse that was waiting for her, and she took off toward the lands of the Dragonoffs.

The mystic had a mission: get as much intel as she could and cause as much damage as she could. It would take her at least two days to get to Valendora.

She came across the village and saw the villagers out and about doing their daily chores and trading. She saw a young boy exiting a hut. He looked up and waved at her. As some of the villagers were acknowledging her, she knew this must have been the home of the woman she shape-shifted into. All she could do was nod and smile.

Arlo came out of the hut, yelling for her to hurry and come

in. He had mistaken her for his mother. She looked over and saw a slight similarity to the one they captured and had escaped. She gave a smile and nodded. She got off the horse and followed him inside.

Arlo was telling her about MJ and how he had escaped and was making his way to Valendora. She looked at him and gave him a smirk. She rested her hand on his shoulder to understand him. Once she did that, she had the vision of MJ talking to him after his escape. Once she fully understood, she let it be known by the blink of her eyes she was a shapeshifter. Her eyes were reptilian and blinked sideways.

The moment he started to scream, she immediately hushed him up. She walked away from the hut, waving her fingers in the air. As she did so, the hut caught on fire.

One of the villagers sounded the horn. Some of the villagers were trying to put the fire out and tried to rescue Arlo but were unable to as the flames quickly engulfed the hut.

A villager approached her, yelling at her and gesturing towards the hut. She grabbed him by his head and twisted it.

The elders pointed at her, yelling, "Diablos! Diablos!"

The mystic gave a smirk and let her eyes go back to reptilian for them to see she was what they called Diablos.

The men in the village were grabbing weapons as the women and children ran from the village. The men started running toward her. She shot flames out her hands, catching them on fire, and sent a few more huts into flames. She turned around and got back up on her horse. She focused on letting her eyes return to normal for the human she had shifted into.

Thousands of Anunnaki were preparing for war. The leader was searching for portals that would bring them closer to Valendora but was not successful in locating one.

The Anunnaki were gathering their armor and weapons and boarding aircraft and horses. Some were simply walking on the journey. They vowed to rid the realm of the humans, Tri-Tyrion, and the Dragonoffs.

Alexis never thought she would have visions, even though it ran in the bloodline on her mother's side. She saw MJ at the gates of Valendora and being turned away. She immediately left Emma and ran out of the palace to the gates.

As she got close to the gates, she yelled up to the guard on the tower watch asking him if anyone tried to enter.

"Yes princess." He chuckled and then said, "He claimed to be your husband. I told him to leave. This was maybe a few minutes ago, headed up the river."

"He is my husband! Open the gates now!" she demanded.

Alexis ran after MJ, yelling for him. He stopped in his tracks when he heard her yelling for him. He turned around and saw her running toward him. He started running towards her. When they reunited, he gave her the biggest hug and kissed her.

"I love you, Alexis. I thought I would never see you again."

"I love you too, MJ! I can't believe you are here! How did you escape?"

"I did what I needed to do to find my way back to you. I left Mother behind. I could only escape myself. I was able to break free through a window and jumped into the river to carry me away. It was the only means I had to escape. It was rough, but I managed."

Alexis started to have another vision. She heard horns blowing and saw the start of the battle at the field where Dresden and Ryn had rescued her from the Kurl.

"MJ, we have to get to my parents now!"

As they returned to the palace, they found her parents, grandparents, and Emma finishing up a conversation in the study with the map pulled out.

"Mom, I started having visions. Just recently, Oh and um, this is my husband MJ."

All of us stood up, shaking his hand and welcoming him into the family. I saw the resemblance of Milledge in him. I know my daughter loves him, but knowing Milledge and Trish, I was unsure. Maybe he was nothing like them, and that I hoped for.

"It is very nice to meet you, MJ. You hurt my daughter. I will be coming after you." Ky said with a stern look on his face.

"Oh, and he would not be the only one, MJ," I said with a chuckle.

"Mom! Dad!" Alexis yelled, embarrassed by them.

"Sorry, hon, we are protective," Ky said, smiling.

Luciana interrupted. "Emma has also had a vision. The war will be starting in one day."

"Yes, and from my vision I had seen a scepter. Break the crystal in the scepter, and there will be no power and no leader for the Anunnaki." Emma chimed in.

"I know where it will be held. It will be in the field where Ryn and Dresden had saved me. They will have many forces. I could not see the outcome." Alexis advised.

Ryn had just shown up to go over strategies. I filled him in on when and where the battle will begin. He immediately left to give Drel and the other Dragonoffs the information. He told me he will make sure they will get set in place prior to us. We had one day to prepare.

"Ky, gather our fighters. I'll get the Minotaurs. I want the women and children in the tunnels. I know since we had been attacked, many had become sickened, and food was scarce. We must do our best to comfort everyone and ration food. The Dragonoffs had helped us as much as they could, but we could not keep counting on them for everything, including our survival. Mom, Dad, and Emma, please help gather those and get them to the shelter. We do not know if the war will move closer to home." I said.

I went to find Nikki and Bray. Nikki became angry after filling them in on everything, and Bray stated he would fight by my side.

She said to him angrily, "I lost someone I loved a long time ago, Bray. I cannot go through that again! I do not want you to go!"

"I will come back to you, Nikki," He promised.

"And I will make sure of it, Nikki," I said.

"I know Jay." She said as we hugged. I assured her everything was going to be alright.

I told Ky that night I did not want him fighting. If anything were to happen to him, I wouldn't want to continue on without him.

I loved him with my heart and soul.

He said he had trained with the Dragonoffs for years, and he was going to fight. He said he was fighting not just for us but for our home, our people, and our future.

A few of the Dragonoffs had arrived at Valendora and would remain in case the battle was to move closer.

MJ was determined to fight and try to get his mother back. Alexis pleaded with him not to go. He insisted.

Alexis had no powers but knew how to fight and insisted on going.

"Alexis, I need for you to stay behind with your grandparents and Emma. If anything were to happen to your father and me, you are the new queen."

"Mother, I am going whether you like it or not. I want to fight alongside you, Dad, and my husband."

"Alexis, listen to your mother. I will be fine, and I will come back to you. I promise." MJ said to her as he hugged her tightly and kissed her softly.

Her eyes filled with tears. She hugged him tightly again. "I lost you once, MJ. I don't want to lose you again."

"You won't my love. I love you more than you could

possibly know. Stay here, and I will return."

Tears came rolling down my face. I looked at Ky and smiled. Their love for each other was much Like Ky and me.

Come morning, we must make our way to the field. The Dragonoffs are already there, cloaked with their invisibility.

Chapter 37

Out of all of us from Valendora that was not sick or told to stay behind, there were about thirty of us. We were small in numbers. The Dragonoffs There were six of them from Drel's clan with their dragons. Word had gotten to the other Dragonoff clans. Two of the clans had backed out; in fear the prophecy would not come to be and did not want any issues with the Anunnaki. The other clan agreed to send a few of their warriors some to Valendora and others to the Anunnaki city to destroy it. They felt the Anunnaki would be sending out all of their warriors, and they were correct. As word got back to them thousands were marching and flying in their crafts toward the boundaries.

MJ looked towards the field. He saw his mother riding a horse from the forest into the field. He yelled out to her and started running toward her. As they met in the middle, she dismounted and walked over toward him. Once he got to her, he gave her a hug. She did not reciprocate. He pulled back looking at her strangely as she always hugged him back. He then noticed her blink and her eyes changing to reptilian. As he was reaching for his knife, she grabbed him by his throat and threw him back towards Jaycenda's small army.

"What the Hell," I said. I used my powers to pick him up and get him back to us in safety.

"That is not my mother." He said with a raspy voice massaging his throat.

I looked up and saw Trish's head tilted. As Ky was helping MJ up, all eyes were focused on Trish. Suddenly, she morphed into the mystic Anunnaki.

"Bane, Axel, Pike, Makeo, go have some fun, boys!" I yelled over to them.

The Minotaurs pounded their chests, reached for their weapons, and gave out their roars.

The Anunnaki were shooting fireballs toward them, but they kept dodging them. They encircled the mystic.

They snorted and growled, communicating with each other. As Pike struck the Anunnaki in the back with his spear, Bane used his sledgehammer, slamming it into the Anunnaki's stomach, pushing the mystic back into the spear further. As it was trying to cast fireballs at them, Axel cut off the hands. As it screamed in agony, Pike pulled out his spear and moved so Makeo could get behind it and chop its head off.

Once that happened, a very loud, deep horn blew three times.

Out of each side of the forest except behind us, the Anunnaki made themselves known. Their crafts came hovering in, shooting lasers at us; we were running and dodging them. Drel and Ryn uncloaked and were taking out the crafts with fire causing debris to fall onto the field and some of the Anunnaki.

Drel had his Dragon breathe fire upon the Anunnaki below. Making their army smaller in size, at least he thought. As more were taken out, more were coming from the forest.

Drel's son Lexor and his dragon uncloaked and joined in burning the Anunnaki. The other Dragonoffs also uncloaked and started taking out more ships that were coming in while Drel and Ryn were burning the Anunnaki. The stench from the burning flesh was unbearable, but it needed to be done.

While the other Dragonoffs changed direction toward the Anunnaki city, along the way, they would continue to burn more Anunnaki and prevent them from entering the Dragonoff's lands. Several ships had surrounded Kane and his dragon and took them down. Kane started fighting with those on the ground and eventually met his end near his dragon. As he and his familiar made eye contact, they closed their eyes, never to awaken.

I was throwing flames at the Anunnaki, teleporting back and forth, trying to confuse them. I then saw the leader he was holding the scepter. I willed the blue fire around me. Ky and the others were fighting those Anunnaki that had avoided the fire attacks from the dragons and my lil balls of fire I was spitting at them. The leader looked over at me and tilted his head. He pounded the scepter into the ground causing the ground to shake. I lost my balance, as did others. I continued to focus.

Thinking that's all he got, I started throwing blue fireballs at him. Somehow, they went right past him and struck others.

He laughed and pointed the scepter towards me, and a beam of light came at me. I dodged it and gave him a smirk.

Another Anunnaki came running toward me. I forced my arms out pushing it back like had I with the bear years ago. As I looked around, we were on the losing side. I couldn't lose hope that we would win this war.

Ryn was taken by surprise. A ship that had not been in the path of Dresden's fire came up flying beside Dresden and Ryn. One of the Anunnaki jumped off the craft and onto Dresden. Ryn and Dresden communicated. While Ryn held onto Dresden's reigns, Dresden flipped over, trying to knock the Anunnaki off him.

Somehow, it was able to hold onto the saddle. Dresden then went in circles, flipping over. Ryn kept looking back, letting his familiar know he was still there. He told him to stop flipping. Once Dresden stopped Ryn stood up and kicked the Anunnaki in the face as it was trying to get up. It took out his weapon and shot Ryn on his left side. Ryn fell off Dresden. Dresden swooped down and grabbed him with his claw and placed him away from the fighting. As the Anunnaki was trying to take command of Dresden, he did another flip and then went sideways between trees, knocking it off him. The Anunnaki got up and started running back into the battle. Dresden burned him and continued to burn more. The Anunnaki was taking everyone out.

With their advanced weapons we were losing some of the Dragonoffs and their dragons. Some retreated while others met their end. Drel's son was among those that been taken out by the Anunnaki. Drel was upset and wanted to grieve but knew he had to focus; this war was the most important war his people would ever have.

I was still holding strong, but I was not sure how much longer I could stop the Anunnaki. There were still many and so few of us. Most of us had been killed. Ky was fighting and using his amazing moves and made some kills, but he was also struck and knocked unconscious. MJ was still fighting but was growing very weak.

Then I heard a voice saying to me, "You are the Arcana of Light. It is time."

Rage took over. I looked over at Ky and saw an Anunnaki over him, holding its weapon over him to finish him off. I pushed my arms out, forcing them away from Ky.

The Minotaurs were having fun killing one Anunnaki after another, they were the strongest and not growing weak.

I braced myself as white light began to glow from me. It surrounded me like it did in the Queen's chamber, only stronger. I arched backwards. Screaming with pain and rage, that light that was coming from me was like a bomb going off for miles. Knocking over the Anunnaki, they were getting up slowly, wondering what had just happened.

As the light continued, I started speaking in a long-forgotten language. Those who were hurt were now healed.

Suddenly Drel and Ryn were screaming in pain. Lexor and the other Dragonoffs somehow managed to come back to life and were screaming in agony. They were growing wings. Wings that were long ago were taken away from them.

They were in amazement and soon flew right beside their familiars fighting. Watching Drel and Ryn teaming up and making moves like acrobats, taking out the Anunnaki was quite the show.

The leader tried to use his scepter and power on me. Bray stood in front of me to protect me and was using his power to fight back. I quickly shielded Bray and I, as the leader, was using more power towards us.

The shield held until the leader focused on Ky. He pointed

his scepter to him, and lighting was coming from it headed toward Ky. I used my powers to push him out of the way.

Bray and I teamed up using our powers on the leader. Drel and Ryn were still teaming up and decided to pick up an Anunnaki one at a time, fly them high above, and drop them into the forest and field, letting the bodies crash into the ground.

Ky and MJ were teaming up against a large, strong Anunnaki; Lexor flew in to assist them. We were starting to be on the winning team.

I could feel my power grow. It felt unbearable. I started chanting again and being lifted off the ground. The light around me was stronger than ever. There was no wind but my hair was blowing out as though I got caught in a strong gust of wind. Balls of light started forming in my hands.

I started throwing them toward the leader. He got hit by a few, stumbling backward, and burn marks appeared on him.

Out of thousands of Anunnaki, only a few remained. I went for the leader. We went back and forth with our powers. Nothing fazed me. He was getting weaker. As I went for the scepter, we both were holding onto it for dear life. Fighting over what may be the downfall of the Anunnaki. As we continued to fight over it, I tried head-butting him, and kicking him. He was not letting go. I finally focused and concentrated on burning the stick of the scepter. It broke in half, and I had the half with the crystal on it. Dresden saw this and hurriedly came down and grabbed me as we flew in a circle around the field. The Anunnaki stopped fighting and were looking up at me as I was standing on Dresden holding half of the scepter with the crystal. I concentrated on the crystal to shatter. It shattered into hundreds of pieces. The look on the Anunnaki's faces, no scepter, no leader. Dresden took me back down to the field. I looked at the former leader he looked at me in disbelief.

As the Anunnaki started to retreat the Minotaurs were chasing after them. I wanted to kill the leader, but I decided to let Drel have that pleasure.

We managed to survive. I had Dresden fly over the Anunnaki city. There was nothing left. No Anunnaki to be seen. The Dragonoffs that went there while the main battle was ongoing, made sure there was nothing left.

The threat of the Anunnaki was no more. We can now go beyond the boundaries and explore this world.

Now that the boundaries are gone, at some point, I would like to try to find a portal to go back to Atlantis to see how Atlantis and Earth have grown since we left. I know there is one, but this is a vast world to explore.

We had celebrated with the Dragonoffs. All of them had their wings regained through my powers; how, I do not know. But they were happy and enjoyed flying beside their familiars.

Two months had passed. The Dragonoffs had started to build cities above ground, knowing there were no more threats to their race. One clan decided to go beyond the boundaries to see where they wanted to settle.

Nikki was very thankful Bray came back to her. They decided to leave Valendora and explore what the world had to offer. Bray swore he would protect her and keep her safe.

We were preparing for back-to-back weddings. Alexis and MJ remarried and had a traditional wedding that she had always dreamed of since she was little. And Emma and Hans had their wedding not long after Alexis. That whole week was filled with the celebration of both unions. Music and feasts, and many tears of joy and lots of laughs. These are the good times to remember.

It was only a few months later that both Alexis and Emma announced they were expecting. Little did Alexis know that I already had a vision and she was going to have a son. A son who would be born with the mark of the intertwined two half-moons.

Who knew there could finally be a world filled with peace? I have my happy ending. A husband who loves me as much as I love him. We loved each other from the moment we met. A daughter who is loved beyond words and a grandchild on the way. Life could not get much better than this.

About The Author

Raylin has always had an interest in writing since she was a child. When she is not writing, she spends time with family and friends. She enjoys traveling and gaining inspiration for her writing.